THE ARTIE CONAN DOYLE MYSTERIES

To Judith, Gem – and Rumble!

Kelpies is an imprint of Floris Books
First published in 2019 by Floris Books
First published in North America in 2020
© 2019 Robert J. Harris

Robert J. Harris has asserted his right under the
Copyright, Designs and Patent Act of 1988 to be
identified as the Author of this Work

This publisher acknowledges subsidy from
Creative Scotland towards the publication
of this volume

 Also available as an eBook

British Library CIP data available
ISBN 978-178250-608-9
Printed in Great Britain by CPI Group (UK) Ltd, Croydon

 Floris Books supports sustainable forest management by
printing this book on materials made from wood that
comes from responsible sources and reclaimed material

MIX
Paper from
responsible sources
FSC® C013604

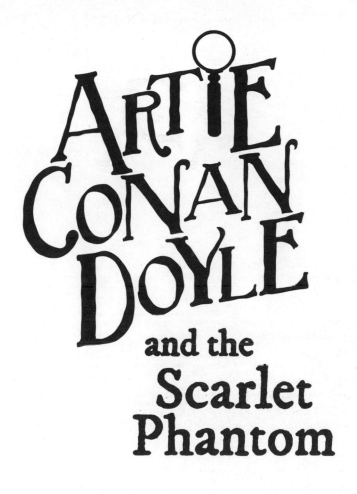

ARTIE CONAN DOYLE

and the
Scarlet
Phantom

ROBERT J. HARRIS

Kelpies

THRILLING
ADVENTURES

ONE PENNY

AUGUST 1873 ISSUE 1

IN THIS ISSUE THE CHILLING MYSTERY OF

The Scarlet Phantom

FEATURING:

Artie Conan Doyle
BOY DETECTIVE

Edward 'Ham' Hamilton
STALWART COMPANION

Peril Abernethy
Girl Scientist

THRILLS! SHOCKS! SUSPENSE!

1.

The Adventures of Beresford Root

Edinburgh, August 1873

"It's a mystery, Artie, a complete mystery," groaned Edward Hamilton.

"What on earth are you talking about, Ham?" asked his friend Artie Conan Doyle.

"I mean how your father can get excited over all those pots and vases," said Ham. "After the first dozen or so my eyes just glaze over."

Mr Charles Altamont Doyle was leading his little party down a long gallery filled with Persian pottery and Venetian glass, providing them with a detailed commentary on each item they passed. His wife Mary was at his side with Artie's two younger sisters, Lottie and Connie, trailing after them. Artie and Ham lagged behind, wishing they could be somewhere else.

"Art is Father's real love," Artie reminded his friend. "His job at the Office of Works is just to pay the bills until his career as an artist begins to flourish."

"It's taking a long time to start flourishing," Ham sighed as Mr Doyle enthused over a decorative honey jar. "He's been in that office for as long as I can remember."

The day had begun much better than this. While the boys were home for the summer from their school, Stonyhurst College, Mr Doyle had decided to take the whole family on a visit to Edinburgh's new Museum of Science and Art in Chambers Street.

Since Mr Doyle was a member of the committee that had approved the new extensions to the museum, he was given a special pass which granted them free entry. It also gave access to areas of the museum that were closed to members of the general public, such as the workshops where skilled artisans constructed detailed models of ships, bridges and steam engines for display.

To the boys the most exciting part of the tour was the great vaulted basement, which was stiflingly hot and filled with a din like the rumblings of an active volcano. Here, huge furnaces boiled hundreds of gallons of water that provided heating for the whole building, and six enormous meters controlled gas that passed to nine thousand burners to light up the multitude of rooms and galleries.

Once they were back up among the public displays,

however, Artie and Ham's interest had soon begun to wane. When Mr Doyle halted before a mosaic of a cypress tree surrounded by weird animals and began explaining the symbolism to his wife and daughters, Ham gave Artie a nudge.

"Let's sneak off and have a bite to eat," he suggested in a whisper.

Artie could see that his mother was doing her best to feign interest in her husband's monologue while the two girls were sitting on the floor playing pat-a-cake. Nobody was going to pay the two of them any attention, so he nodded and followed Ham down a corridor of textiles imported from all over the world. They ducked through an archway and found themselves in a broad chamber devoted to geology.

Bypassing a row of glass cases filled with anthracite, bitumen, bauxite and other minerals, they sat themselves down on one of the benches that ran up the centre of the room. Ham reached into his pocket and unwrapped a slice of carrot cake, which he began to devour.

"I swear if I have to stare at one more vase," he grumbled through a mouthful of cake, "I shall probably pass out."

"One day I am sure that my father's own art will begin to sell," said Artie. "In the meantime I've been wondering how I can make some money to contribute to the household. What with Father's bouts of ill health, we always seem to come up short."

"Another mystery or two would do the trick," Ham commented glumly. "It seems like forever since Professor Anderson hired us to investigate the strange goings on at his magic show."

It had been the previous summer that this adventure had taken place, and even longer since they had investigated the theft of dead bodies from Edinburgh's graveyards. Since then both boys had found school and home life increasingly humdrum.

"I suppose there aren't really that many mysteries around," said Artie, "especially ones somebody would pay a couple of schoolboys to investigate."

"My mother still wants me to be a musician," moaned Ham. "She's threatening to buy me a glockenspiel. I've no idea what that is, but it sounds beastly."

Artie slid a notebook out of his pocket and began to riffle through the pages. "Do you remember when you had a go at writing an account of our run-in with the Gravediggers' Club and then gave up?"

"Do I?" Ham groaned. "That first page was hard enough, getting all those words in the right order. Then I kept making a mess with the ink. How anyone can stand to write a whole book is beyond me."

"Well, I thought I would give it a try," Artie confided.

"You know, since the newspapers never told the whole story. Perhaps a magazine would publish it if I dressed it up as a piece of fiction."

"You really should stick to the facts," Ham advised. "I know you, Artie. You won't be able to resist throwing in some pirates and a centaur."

Artie gave an exasperated snort. "Well, I've made a start. Do you want to hear it?"

Ham searched his pockets but could find nothing else to eat. He shrugged. "I suppose so."

Artie held the notebook open in front of him and read.

"The fog was rolling in from the river as investigative agent Beresford Root made his way through the dark graveyard. At his side was his stalwart companion, the portly seaman Odysseus Plank."

"Portly?" Ham exclaimed. "You're not suggesting I'm portly, are you?"

"No, no, of course not," Artie responded hurriedly. "I'm quite sure that almost nobody would ever describe you as portly. Odysseus Plank is a fictional character, remember."

"And what about those names? Beresford Prune?"

"Not Prune, Root," Artie corrected. "Because he gets to the root of the problem. And Odysseus Plank is a perfect name for a sailor."

Ham tutted like a disappointed teacher. "Artie, real people don't have ridiculous names like those. What are you going to call this story anyway?"

"I thought I would call it *The Adventure of the Disappearing Dead.*"

"Oh no, that's far too creepy." Ham shuddered. "Nobody but a ghoul would want to read a story like that. You need to give it a cheery title if you want to attract readers."

"A cheery title?" Artie echoed dubiously.

Ham furrowed his brow in thought, casting his mind back to that first adventure they had shared together. Then, raising a triumphant finger, he announced, "*How a Cake Saved the Day.* That's what actually happened, after all. There, you can use that for a title and I won't even charge you for it."

"I'm very grateful, I'm sure," Artie responded sourly. "I suppose you'd like me to begin the tale in a bakery."

"I say, that's not a bad idea," Ham enthused. Then he paused and shook his head. "Still, I wouldn't waste my time if I were you."

"Oh, you wouldn't?"

"Everybody knows that writers don't make any money," Ham declared sagely. "They only stick at it because they're cracked in the head."

"Do you think you two could stifle your chatter?" a girl's voice interrupted. "I am trying to concentrate."

Artie leaned forward to see past Ham, to where a girl was seated further up the bench with a sketch pad in her lap.

She was wearing a short-brimmed hat of plaited straw, a walking suit of brown tweed, and a pair of stout, unladylike boots. Her straight brown hair was cut short in the style of a pageboy in a medieval painting. Sharp grey eyes framed in steel-rimmed spectacles peered sternly back at him over a small button nose. Apparently satisfied that she had made her point, she returned to her drawing.

Artie got up and made his way over to where she was sitting. Tilting his head, he examined her pad. "What is it you're drawing here? It looks like a lot of squiggles."

"I'm making a sketch of that fossil," the girl told him brusquely. She pointed her pencil towards a nearby glass cabinet where a flat piece of grey stone was on display, its surface imprinted with lines like herringbones.

Joining them, Ham glanced back and forth between the drawing and the geological sample. "Fossil? It just looks like a lump of rock to me."

The girl treated him to a scornful glare. "It is all that remains of *Eozoön canadense*, a creature that lived upon the earth long before recorded history."

"That must have been an awfully long time ago," said Artie, attempting to be pleasant.

"With every new geological discovery," the girl informed him, "it becomes ever clearer that the earth is far, far older than anyone ever imagined." She sounded very proud of this fact, as if she had made all those discoveries herself.

"Artie, you don't suppose it's even older than Father Flynn, do you?" Ham joked.

"Father Flynn?" echoed the girl, wrinkling her small nose.

"He's one of the teachers at our school," Artie explained. "He looks so old some people say he learned all about botany in the Garden of Eden and was first mate aboard Noah's Ark."

The girl was about to say something when she was interrupted by the clumping of heavy footsteps. Artie and Ham looked up to see their policeman friend George McCorkle striding towards them with a folded newspaper tucked under his arm. He was dressed in a dark grey suit with a bowler hat perched on his head and a pair of leather brogues on his feet. His bushy moustache twitched in the suggestion of a smile.

"Ah, Mr Conan Doyle – the very fellow I was looking for. And here is your associate, Mr Henderson."

"Hamilton," Ham corrected him, with a vexed frown.

"Exactly," McCorkle agreed, as though he hadn't made a mistake at all.

At a gesture from the policeman, they followed him away from the geological exhibit, glad to be leaving the girl with the annoyingly superior manner.

"It's very good to see you, Sergeant McCorkle," Artie remarked as they moved out along a gallery of zoological specimens. "I must say it's strange to find you not in uniform."

Puffing out his chest, McCorkle declared proudly, "That's Inspector McCorkle. And now that I am an inspector, I no longer wear a constable's uniform but have been provided with this very smart police detective's suit."

Artie and Ham had found McCorkle to be a very slow, plodding sort of policeman, even though there was no doubting his good intentions. Trying hard to sound sincere, Artie said, "Congratulations, Inspector. I'm sure the promotion is well deserved."

"Yes, well deserved," Ham muttered under his breath.

"As you are aware," said McCorkle, "I have played a crucial role in one or two highly important cases, such as the graveyard robberies and the case of the Vanishing Dragon. It was my sterling work in those matters that led to my new rank."

Artie's jaw dropped. Actually he and Ham had solved both the cases McCorkle referred to – and defeated the villains in the process. The full facts, however, had been covered up in the newspapers and the names of the two boys had not even been mentioned. All the credit had gone to McCorkle, who had made the final arrests.

"I think Ham and I played some part in those cases," Artie reminded him.

"You were indeed of some assistance," McCorkle conceded, "and I expect that if you were to become better acquainted with proper police procedures, you might one day make a capable pair of constables."

Ham let out an exasperated gasp. "Constables? Why, we're already better detectives than – ouch!"

Artie had elbowed his friend sharply in the ribs to silence him. "What Ham is saying is that we've learned so much from working with you that we're already most of the way there." He knew that the policeman's goodwill might be valuable to them in the future, so he didn't want Ham puncturing the inspector's high opinion of himself.

"Well, Mr Doyle," said McCorkle with a slow nod, "I will admit that though your methods may be eccentric, they do on occasion yield results. In fact, I would go so far as to say that, in spite of your wild flights of fancy, you have something of a knack for stumbling into the right place at the right time."

"It's very kind of you to say so," Artie responded politely.

Rubbing his bruised ribs, Ham glowered at his friend. "Yes, very kind," he muttered in a tone that was considerably less polite.

"Which brings me to the matter at hand," said the policeman, raising a dramatic eyebrow. With a furtive gesture he beckoned to the boys to follow him into a secluded corner behind a large stuffed polar bear. Once he was sure they were out of sight of prying eyes, he unfolded his copy of today's *Scotsman* newspaper and presented it to Artie.

"I wondered if you might have some insights into this particular business. It appears we are confronted by…" – the inspector hesitated and Artie was sure he gave a shudder – "by an invisible menace."

2.

The Mystery of the Invisible Robber

The policeman pointed sombrely to an article in the upper right-hand corner of the newspaper. The two boys crowded together to see it. Peering closely, Artie began reading out loud:

THE SCOTSMAN

MYSTERY OF THE INVISIBLE ROBBER

◆

At approximately midday on Monday, August 11th, the streets of Edinburgh bore witness (if 'witness' is the correct word under such circumstances) to the most extraordinary and inexplicable crime in the city's long and colourful history. A prominent diamond merchant, Mr Royston Kincaid of Kincaid Jewellers, George Street, was walking along that very road when he was suddenly seized, thrust against a wall then knocked to the ground. This assault was carried out by an assailant who was entirely invisible both to Mr Kincaid and to the several passers-by who observed the incident with understandable incredulity. Two of them rushed to the stricken man's aid and helped him to his feet. Upon searching his pockets, Mr Kincaid discovered that he had been robbed of a valuable necklace he had been on his way to deliver to a wealthy client.

Several of the witnesses accompanied Mr Kincaid to the Police Office, where he stated that he saw no assailant, yet he had been both assaulted and robbed. The astonished witnesses confirmed the veracity of Mr Kincaid's account.

The matter has been placed in the capable hands of the recently promoted Inspector George McCorkle, who has a reputation for solving the most unusual crimes and arresting the most elusive of villains. Perhaps he can shed light on these shocking events.

"Well, that's a whopper of a mystery!" said Ham.

The two boys turned to the inspector, who was tugging at his bushy moustache in an agitated manner.

"Do you have any clues, Inspector?" Artie asked.

McCorkle shook his head unhappily. "I confess, Mr Doyle, that I find myself quite at sea with regard to this business. My first thought was that it must be a hoax, that this Kincaid concocted this fictitious crime. However, a number of completely reliable witnesses swear they saw him being knocked about."

"And if he wanted to fake a robbery in order to keep the necklace for himself," said Artie, "why would he not just stage a burglary in his shop? This ludicrous notion of an invisible man is bound to draw attention to him."

"Exactly my thinking," the inspector concurred gloomily. "And yet there are only these two options: that Mr Kincaid has staged a false robbery of the most impossible kind, for reasons that can hardly be guessed at, or that there is an invisible thief abroad on the streets of Edinburgh."

"An invisible thief!" Ham gave a low whistle. "What a corker!"

Artie slid a hand into his pocket to finger his notebook, hoping to gain some inspiration from his fictional detective, Beresford Root. Nothing sprang to mind, however. "I can't say that I have any other ideas, Inspector," he said. "What is it you want me to do?"

"Well, given your experience with what I might call the more outlandish class of crime," McCorkle began gruffly, "and that your methods lie outside the bounds of traditional police work, I would appreciate it if you would make inquiries of your own and share with me any information you unearth." From inside his jacket he pulled out a blank envelope and handed it to Artie. "Here is a document which will smooth your way."

Artie opened the envelope and took out a single sheet of paper, which he read with Ham peering over his shoulder.

The bearer of this letter, Mr Arthur Conan Doyle, in spite of his youth, has been of great assistance to the police in previous investigations. I would ask therefore that you give him your fullest cooperation in this particular matter. I can vouch for both his character and his discretion.

Inspector George McCorkle,
Edinburgh Constabulary

"Why doesn't it mention me?" Ham grumbled under his breath.

Oblivious to the remark, McCorkle raised a cautionary eyebrow. "I would ask you to use this document sparingly, Mr Doyle, and to keep your involvement in this case confidential."

"Yes, of course," Artie assured him.

"In that case I will bid you good day," said the inspector with a tip of his hat. "I have crimes of the more conventional sort to deal with, such as a stolen bicycle and a drunken affray at the docks."

And with that he stomped off.

"I say, that's a bit thick, isn't it?" said Ham, scowling after the inspector. "Expecting us to solve the crime for him but keeping our part in it a secret."

"We're a long way from solving it," said Artie with a frown.

"Indeed you are," interjected a voice, "and that's because you aren't approaching it scientifically."

The boys turned sharply to see a slight figure emerge from its hiding place behind a stuffed albatross. It was the annoying girl from the geology chamber.

"What are you doing sneaking about after us?" Artie challenged, wondering how she had managed to creep up on them unobserved.

"Yes, did you get tired of drawing rocks?" added Ham.

"Fossils," the girl corrected him tersely. "When I saw you being led off by a policeman, my interest was piqued, and when something piques my interest, I pursue it. That is how discoveries are made."

"Look, who are you anyway?" Artie demanded.

"My name," the girl declared, as though it were

something to be proud of, "is Miss Peril Abernethy."

"Pearl?" said Artie. "You mean like the precious gem?"

"Indeed not," the girl asserted. "I spell it P-E-R-I-L, Peril meaning danger."

"And Abernethy is—" Ham began.

"Yes, like the Abernethy biscuit," Peril interrupted testily. "And who are you two that a reputable police officer should ask for your help?"

Artie drew himself up and tried to look as noble as possible. "My name," he informed her, "is Arthur Ignatius Conan Doyle, Arthur as in the famous king, Ignatius from the noted saint, Conan from—"

"Yes, yes, that's quite enough of that," Peril cut in. "Anybody can give himself a really long name if he puts his mind to it. It doesn't prove anything."

"Neither does being named after a dangerous biscuit," Artie retorted. He grinned as if he had just scored a goal in a school football match.

"My name is Edward Hamilton," Ham put in. Feeling that to be rather inadequate, he added, "Esquire – and gentleman of this parish."

"Very grand, I'm sure," said Peril. "Still, I can't see what resources you can bring to this investigation. Why, I don't suppose you could tell graphite from anthracite, or bitumen from resin."

"I can't see why we'd want to," Ham huffed. "Rocks

23

are rocks, and we can find better things to do with our time than giving them names."

"Really?" Peril raised a supercilious eyebrow. "No wonder you appear so appallingly ignorant."

"Ignorant!" Artie exploded. "I'll have you know we are pupils at Stonyhurst College."

"The noted Jesuit school in Lancashire," Ham added proudly.

"Oh, I see, it's run by priests, is it?" said Peril. "I suppose they fill your head with a lot of fairy tales and stuff about angels dancing on needles instead of teaching you proper science."

"We learn about God, if that's what you mean," Artie retorted brusquely, "but we learn all of the sciences as well."

"The school even has its own observatory," Ham informed her, "which was used in the great magnetic survey of 1858."

"In fact," said Artie, "Jesuit astronomers developed the system used for classifying stars and were the first to describe the canals on Mars."

Peril waved a hand at him to keep him from carrying on. "Yes, yes, I'm sure some of them are quite clever, but it's still not the same as a proper scientific education."

"What is that supposed to mean?" demanded Ham.

"I was not farmed out to some far-off school run by strangers," Peril declared haughtily. "My parents, both noted experts in the fields of geology and chemistry, chose to educate me at home. In addition, I have received instruction from a series of private tutors, such as Dr Pierre Lafarge the noted mathematician and Madame Evangeline Drussler the renowned botanist."

"You mean you sit at home all day while people come and teach you things?" said Artie.

"Not at all. We make regular field trips to places of interest to seek out rare insects and fossils."

"Well, why don't you go and find some bugs?" Artie suggested, slipping McCorkle's letter of introduction into his pocket. "We have business to attend to. Come on, Ham, we should have a word with this fellow Kincaid."

The boys headed for the main hallway with Peril stalking along behind them.

"You won't get anywhere as long as you're prepared to swallow a lot of fantastical tosh about an invisible man," she advised them. "You might as well suppose the crime was carried out by a genie who flew off on a magic carpet."

"Stranger things have happened," Ham countered without thinking.

"Oh really?" said Peril. "Such as?"

"Well, such as, as…" Ham found himself stuck for a reply.

Before Artie could come up with one, his parents emerged from an adjoining gallery with his two sisters in tow. Lottie and Connie scampered off among some statues while their mother pursued them, half cross and half amused.

"Artie, where did you and Ham wander off to?" his father asked mildly.

"Er… we were looking at the fossils," Artie answered. He didn't want to say anything about McCorkle.

"They're rocks with dead animals in them," Ham explained.

"Well, we're all going for lunch now," said Mr Doyle, "so come along."

Artie and Ham exchanged glances. They couldn't say they were off to investigate a bizarre crime, but they wanted to head over to the jeweller's before the trail grew any colder.

"We were going to… er… um…" Artie mumbled.

"That is," said Ham, "we thought… er…"

Peril intervened decisively. "Actually, they're coming with me."

The Sign of the Clutching Hand

Mr Doyle gazed at the girl curiously, noting her unusually practical clothing. Peril Abernethy peered up at him through her steel-rimmed spectacles. "I offered to show them my private collection of rare minerals. I only live a few streets away and they seem very keen."

"I'll say," said Ham, failing to sound enthusiastic.

"Yes, this is Miss Biscuit," Artie explained. Ignoring Peril's indignant hiss, he added, "I know she looks very young, but it seems she's quite the expert on rocks and whatever you might find inside them."

"Well, I suppose it is educational," his father conceded, rubbing his jaw thoughtfully.

"Yes, very," Peril affirmed. "I have several fascinating examples of feldspar and mica." Placing a hand on the back of each of the boys, she pushed them towards the museum exit with surprising strength.

"We won't be long," Artie called back over his shoulder as they were bundled out the door. "We'll catch up with you."

As they descended the stone steps to the street, Ham grumbled, "I hope this is worth missing lunch for."

"The sooner we begin investigating the better," said Artie, pausing to get his bearings. He turned to Peril. "Thanks for giving us an excuse to get away."

"You don't have to thank me," said Peril tartly, "but you might have the courtesy to get my name right. Miss Biscuit indeed!"

"I'm sorry," said Artie. "I was caught off guard and all I could remember was you saying 'like the biscuit'."

"Never mind," said Peril, shrugging the issue aside. "What's done is done. Now, are we going to tackle this mystery or aren't we?"

"I don't recall anybody inviting you to be a part of it," Artie pointed out. "It looks like a very challenging case."

He and Ham set off down the street and he was somewhat put out to find Peril marching briskly alongside him.

"That is why you need my help," she said. "When one wishes to solve a problem, one needs to think scientifically. The first thing one must do is eliminate the impossible – and an invisible man is utterly impossible."

"Alright then," Artie challenged, "if you're so clever, how do you explain it?"

"The answer is very likely meteorological," Peril declared primly.

"Meteor-what?" said Ham.

"You mean it has something to do with the weather?" said Artie.

"Correct, Doyle," said Peril with a bob of her head. "A sudden jump in temperature or an abrupt shift of air pressure might form a small whirlwind, which would buffet a man this way and that, so it would appear he was being assaulted."

"Would that be enough to throw him against a wall?" Artie was sceptical.

"Certainly," said Peril. "A strong gust of wind can easily knock a man off his feet. It happens all the time."

"Hang on," Ham objected. "What about the stolen necklace?"

"Oh, it probably just fell out of his pocket," said Peril.

"But then he would have spotted it, wouldn't he?" said Ham.

"Not if it was snatched up by one of the witnesses," said Artie thoughtfully. "There were a number of people on the scene and any one of them might have been tempted to grab something so valuable."

"There, crime solved!" Peril concluded.

"That is just a theory," Artie cautioned. "We still need to talk to the victim."

As they walked on, Ham leaned in close to his friend and murmured, "I say, Artie, if old McCorkle finds out she cracked the case in a matter of minutes, we're going to look pretty daft, aren't we?"

"Let's just have a word with Mr Kincaid," said Artie calmly. In fact, however, he was just as horrified as Ham at the notion that this girl, who had popped up out of nowhere, might have solved the case before they had even started their investigation.

When they reached George Street the broad thoroughfare was busy with shoppers, most of them well-dressed women. They passed a milliner's window crammed with expensive hats, a tobacconist's from which a smoky scent wafted, and a pharmacy dispensing all manner of medicines.

Ham gave a vigorous sniff. "I smell fresh bread! There must be a bakery nearby."

"Yes, it's just up there," said Peril pointing ahead.

"Look, there's the jeweller's on the other side of the road," said Artie.

A horse-drawn omnibus rumbled by as they crossed over and paused in front of Kincaid's establishment.

"Look, I'd better go in myself," said Artie. "McCorkle's letter only vouches for me, and he might not be willing to talk if there's a whole gang of us."

"That's fine," Ham agreed, eyeing the bakery on the other side of the road. "It will give me a chance to have a bit of lunch before I shrivel away into a fossil."

"Alright, Doyle," Peril agreed testily. "But make sure you interrogate him thoroughly. His story is bound to crumble under scrutiny."

A bell rang above the door as Artie entered the jeweller's shop, and a dark-haired woman with rabbity teeth looked up from rearranging some necklaces in one of the display cases. Taking in Artie's schoolboy appearance, she said, "I don't believe we have anything in your price range, young man. This isn't a toy shop."

Artie drew himself up to his full height, trying to look and sound as adult as possible. "I'm here to see Mr Kincaid on a matter of great importance."

"Mr Kincaid is busy in the rear office right now. Can I do something for you?"

"Thank you, but no," said Artie. "I need to speak to him privately." Seeing her expression harden, he added, "It's extremely urgent, and he really will want to hear what I have to say."

The woman blinked. "Well, I suppose in that case Mr Kincaid can spare you a moment."

Retreating behind the counter, she rapped on a frosted glass door at the rear of the shop. A moment later, the door was opened by a portly, middle-aged man dressed in a dark blue suit with a heavy gold watch chain spanning his waistcoat. With mild displeasure, he said, "Miss Toner?"

"I'm sorry to interrupt, Mr Kincaid," said the woman, "but this boy claims to have urgent business with you."

From behind Kincaid a wiry young man in a loud checked suit popped into view, brandishing a notebook and pencil. A second pencil was stuck through the band of his hat and two more protruded from his breast pocket. The young man's nose was as pointed as his pencil and beneath it his small ginger moustache twitched like he was trying to repress a sneeze.

"Oho! 'Urgent business', is it?" he exclaimed. "Another exclusive, eh? Let's have it then, sonny."

His beady blue eyes were so intense Artie took an involuntary step backwards. "And who might you be?"

"Name's Ferryman, Johnny Ferryman. Folks in the business call me the Ferret."

"I'm sure they do," said Artie. "And the business is…?"

"News, sonny, news. Reporter for the *Scotsman* newspaper, that's me. Top reporter, if I can blow my own trumpet for a minute."

"What is this business you want to talk to me about?" Kincaid the jeweller asked in a slow, ponderous voice.

Aware that the reporter had his pencil poised to record his words, Artie said, "That's highly confidential, sir."

"Oh, tight-lipped are we?" Ferryman chuckled. "Well, I expect you're just having a lark, eh?" He flipped his notebook shut and brandished it in the air as he scuttled towards the door. "Never mind, I've got plenty here to rush into the evening edition."

As soon as the reporter was gone, Kincaid waved Artie inside. Miss Toner closed the door and returned to the front of the shop.

The jeweller eyed Artie suspiciously. "If you have anything important to say to me, boy, then spit it out. I don't have all day."

"Actually, sir, I'm here to help you recover your stolen necklace." Artie handed over McCorkle's letter of introduction. "If you'll just read this."

Kincaid scanned the note then handed it back with a growl. "Sending boys to investigate is hardly standard procedure."

"It is a very unusual case," said Artie, "so the inspector is prepared to employ every resource."

"I already told the police all about the incident." Kincaid treated Artie to an impatient scowl. "I was struck twice by an unseen hand, then I was seized and slammed into the wall. While I lay on the ground stunned, the necklace intended for Lady Gladgrove was removed from my pocket. A number of witnesses have given statements testifying to these events."

"I don't suppose it's possible," Artie suggested hesitantly, "that you were buffeted by a strong wind, perhaps even a whirlwind? Apparently such things do happen."

"Don't be absurd!" the jeweller snapped. "I know when I've been attacked. Besides, I now have proof that I am the victim of some cunning fiend."

"Proof?"

"Miss Toner came upon a card that was slipped under the door yesterday morning before we opened. Thinking it a joke, she put it away in a drawer among her papers and forgot about it. Only when she came upon it today did she realise that it might be connected to these extraordinary events."

He pointed to the object in question, which lay on the desk in front of him. It was a blank business card on which a brief message had been written in red ink:

You will be my
first victim
at noon today

Artie felt a chill in his blood as he gazed down at the small, neat handwriting. The sinister skeletal hand seemed to suggest the evil intent of some devilish being.

4.

The Second Warning

"I must assume that this note was meant as a warning," said Kincaid, "and it is only through the incompetence of my assistant that I did not receive it until today."

"Yes, it can't be a coincidence," Artie agreed. "This must have been written by the unseen robber."

"Exactly. I was just about to take it to the police," said the jeweller, picking up the card, "when that reporter chap showed up wanting a first-hand account of the whole ordeal. He made a copy of the message and the drawing in his notepad, so I expect it will soon be in the papers."

"Look, I have to report to the inspector anyway," said Artie. "Why don't I take this card to him and save you the bother?"

Kincaid patted his waistcoat thoughtfully. "I have already spent enough time with the police and I have pressing work to be getting on with. I suppose, since the police appear to trust you…"

He handed the card over and Artie tucked it away in the envelope along with McCorkle's letter. "I'd best hurry straight to the Police Office. I'll be sure to tell the inspector exactly how it came into your possession, sir."

Artie had the impression that the jeweller was relieved not to have any more contact with the police. He headed outside, ignoring a disapproving glare from Miss Toner. In front of the shop Peril was pacing impatiently while Ham had made a visit to the bakery on the other side of the road and was munching on a fresh teacake.

"Well? Did you pick his absurd story full of holes?" the girl inquired.

"Not exactly," said Artie. He took out the mysterious card and showed it to the other two. "This was slipped under the door early yesterday morning but had been mislaid until now."

"I say, that hand is a bit creepy!" Ham mumbled through a mouthful of teacake.

"It's definitely a clue," said Artie.

"Extraordinary!" Peril exclaimed. She took the card and examined it through a magnifying glass she whipped out of her skirt pocket.

"It's not written in blood, is it?" Ham wondered.

Peril sniffed the card then peered at it again through the glass. "No, it's ordinary red ink, and you can purchase this type of card at any stationer's."

"Well, so much for your whirlwind theory," said Artie. "I don't think the wind leaves a calling card."

"Or gives advance warning of its intentions," Ham added with a hint of smugness.

Peril fumed for a moment before shoving the card back into Artie's hand. "Then it must be a hoax!"

"But what would be the point?" Artie objected. "Why should anyone make up an absurd story about an invisible man?"

"Because there is something wrong with his brain," Peril countered stubbornly. "Perhaps in the street he suffered from a seizure that caused him to convulse in such a violent fashion that it appeared as though he were being manhandled by an unseen assailant."

"But the man himself claimed he was attacked," Artie insisted.

Peril planted her hands on her hips. "Obviously if his brain had become disordered then his perceptions too would be affected, rendering his testimony quite worthless. This entire business is a fantasy of his unbalanced mind."

"And the card?"

"He wrote it himself, of course, perhaps while sleepwalking."

Ham swallowed the last bite of teacake and licked the crumbs from his fingers. "I don't know. This story of yours sounds even harder to believe than an invisible man."

"We'll see about that," Peril asserted stubbornly. "I'm going to find a text book on disorders of the brain and get to the bottom of this." She handed Artie a card with her address on it. "Come and see me tomorrow and I'll prove to you that it can all be explained quite logically."

With that, she turned and marched away.

Ham shook his head. "Artie, I know you've come up with some crazy notions, but that girl really takes the biscuit."

"At least she's got some ideas," said Artie. "I have to confess that I'm stumped. Come on, we'd best take this new evidence to the inspector."

On the way, Ham recalled gloomily that he had to go home for his piano lessons. "Come and see me in the morning," he said as the friends parted. "Maybe we can take Berrybus for a walk." Berrybus, Ham's enormous black dog, required lots of regular exercise.

The Police Office was off the High Street, at the top of Old Fishmarket Close. When Artie arrived, there was a buzz of excitement going on. McCorkle had left word with the desk sergeant that Artie was to be brought straight to his office when he appeared.

In his office, McCorkle was deep in conversation with a broad-shouldered man whose round florid face was topped by a mane of long white hair. When Artie entered, he broke off.

"Ah, Mr Doyle, have you brought me anything of use?"

"I believe so, Inspector. Mr Kincaid has just come into possession of a warning he received yesterday morning but was mislaid until now."

"A warning?" McCorkle's eyebrows shot up.

"Yes, sir." Artie handed over the card with its red lettering and threatening image.

The inspector's eyes grew wide and he turned to the white-haired man. "Well, this casts a new and troubling light on your business, Mr Seaton."

Seaton eyed the card and Artie heard him grind his teeth. "So, Inspector, is this directly related to that extraordinary crime I read about in the paper this morning?"

"It would appear so," McCorkle affirmed. "Mr Doyle, this is Mr Reginald Seaton, the prominent textile importer. Mr Seaton, this young fellow has been running some errands for me, and I have learned by experience that he has an occasional insight into the ways of crime. Might you show him the item you have brought in?"

Seaton treated Artie to a dubious glare, then opened his hand to display a card. It was identical in size to the one Artie had just handed the inspector and also contained a message in red ink.

You will be my second victim at ten o'clock tonight

The handwriting and the sign of the clutching hand were identical to those on the card Kincaid the jeweller had received.

Artie gasped as a surge of excitement filled his chest. This second card meant Peril's theories were wrong. There really must be some fiend at work.

"How was this delivered to you, if you don't mind my asking?" Artie inquired.

Seaton pursed his lips. "It was the strangest thing. After breakfast, I entered my study as usual and found this lying on my desk on top of my papers. I questioned my secretary Hubert Simpkin, who swore he had not placed it there and that no one else had entered or left the house all morning."

"Unless they entered and left unseen." Artie's voice was hushed.

41

McCorkle cleared his throat uneasily. "Tell me, Mr Seaton, are you acquainted with Mr Kincaid the jeweller?"

"I'd never even heard of the chap until I saw his name in this morning's paper," said Seaton. "I had not connected that robbery with the prank someone is playing on me – not until now."

"I suspect it is more than a prank, Mr Seaton," McCorkle stated gravely. "One robbery has already been committed and it appears you are to be the target of a similar crime."

"Bosh!" Seaton scoffed. "It is clearly a piece of nonsense, a jape of some sort. I was half-minded not to report it, but Simpkin insisted. He's a nervy chap and easily frightened by such things."

"But you do have items of value that would be of interest to the thief?" the inspector inquired.

"I keep my cash in the bank," Seaton replied. "My house contains a few antiques, the silverware and my business papers."

A sudden thought struck Artie. "Do you keep any jewels in your home?"

"Why, yes," the businessman replied. "I recently purchased some rubies from a contact in India, as an investment, you know."

"I take it they are secured," said the inspector.

"They are locked away in a safe in my study," Seaton

responded stiffly, "a safe to which only I have the combination. No thief, invisible or otherwise, is going to get at them."

"Nevertheless," said the inspector, "I believe it would be prudent for you to have a police guard, just for tonight."

"I do not care to have a crowd of bobbies tramping all over my new carpets," growled the merchant.

"It will just be myself and a constable," McCorkle assured him, "and young Mr Doyle here."

"Very well then." Seaton was grudging. He snatched up his hat and headed out the door. "I shall expect you at seven. And please be discreet."

Once the merchant was gone, McCorkle approached Artie in a conspiratorial manner.

"I would be grateful if you could make yourself available this evening, Mr Doyle. This is a rum business, and the more eyes we have about the place the better."

"Why, yes, of course," said Artie. But, in fact, he was rather worried what his parents would say when he told them he was on the trail of an invisible robber.

5.

The Locked Room

Back home at Sciennes Hill Place, Artie picked his way through his supper, trying to work up the nerve to tell his parents about his new investigation. They knew he had been involved in two mysteries before and were happy that the police had kept this a secret from the public. His mother in particular was concerned that no scandal should arise from a member of the family being involved with graveyards and mysterious events.

Once his two sisters had been tucked into bed, he finally broke the news.

"An invisible robber?" said his father. "Yes, I read about it in the paper. But what has that to do with you?"

"Inspector McCorkle thinks I might have some ideas, spot a few clues, that sort of thing."

"It sounds to me like the work of an unclean spirit," said his mother, crossing herself for protection against evil. "The thing to do is bring Father Mulholland in to exorcise it."

"I think it's a bit early to be calling in the Church, Mary," Mr Doyle objected.

"Yes, we don't really know what we're dealing with yet." Artie was horrified at the thought of bringing their local priest in to splash holy water around.

His mother wagged a warning finger. "Well, whether it's a spiritual force or just some trickery, it sounds far too dangerous for you to be poking your nose in."

"The inspector will be there with one of his constables," said Artie. "Besides, the only one being threatened is this Mr Seaton, and with us there to scare the bandit off, nothing might happen."

"I suppose if the police are on the scene and they really want your help," said Mr Doyle, "then we shouldn't stand in the way of the law." There was just a hint of pride in his voice that the Edinburgh Constabulary placed such confidence in his son.

There was a knock at the front door, and when they opened it they saw a constable standing stiffly to attention. He was a fair-haired young man whose large ears stuck out below a sturdy policeman's helmet of the type that had recently replaced the old-fashioned top hat. He wore a long, dark blue coat and a leather belt from which hung a truncheon and a lantern.

"I'm Constable Peter Pennycook," he explained. "Inspector McCorkle sent me to fetch young Master Doyle."

45

While Artie donned his coat and cap, his mother told the constable to keep a close eye on her son and see that no harm befell him.

"It's not too late to arrange for a priest to be on hand," she advised him.

"I don't think there's any call for that, ma'm," Pennycook answered politely, "but I will pass on your advice to the inspector."

As they headed down the tenement stairs, Artie wished that Ham could be here with him, and even that rather trying girl, but Inspector McCorkle insisted that it would only provoke the already ill-tempered Mr Seaton to have a trio of youngsters invading his house.

A horse-drawn cab was waiting. Once they were both inside and on their way, the young constable removed his helmet and scratched his head.

"The inspector seems to lay great store by your abilities, Mr Doyle."

Artie shrugged. "I think I just get lucky sometimes."

"In my opinion, doggedness is the most important quality in a policeman," said Constable Pennycook. "The ability to stick with an investigation and see it through to the end."

"You could well be right," said Artie with more conviction than he felt.

Pennycook replaced his helmet and sighed. "Still, I

don't expect anything will happen tonight. This invisible man business must be some sort of practical joke."

"Do you really think so?"

"You'd be surprised how often people waste police time with shenanigans." The constable allowed himself a small chuckle. "Why, one time I had to stand guard over a woman who claimed there were Cossacks in fur hats climbing around in the trees at the back of her house. Turns out they were just squirrels and she'd been drinking too much gin."

Shortly thereafter they arrived at a handsome two-storey house in Regent Terrace. It was surrounded by a large garden and several beech trees. Once they had climbed out of the cab, the constable led the way up the front path. When they knocked on the door, they were admitted by a pale little man who twitched nervously as he showed them into the parlour. Artie assumed he was Hubert Simpkin, the secretary whom Seaton had spoken of earlier.

Some new development appeared to have upset the merchant and the inspector was trying unsuccessfully to calm him.

"Are you trying to make a comedy of this?" Seaton waved his evening paper under McCorkle's nose.

When the inspector made no reply, Constable Pennycook intervened in support of his chief.

"I think comedy is putting it rather strongly, sir," he protested mildly.

"You think so?" Seaton rounded on him and thrust the newspaper at the young policeman. "Just have a look at this!"

The constable took the paper and he and Artie peered at it. It was a copy of the *Edinburgh Evening News*, a new title which the publishers of the *Scotsman* had launched only a few weeks ago. It was folded open at the main story of the day and the headline read:

WHO IS THE SCARLET PHANTOM?

◆

The article repeated that morning's *Scotsman* account of the attack on Kincaid, adding the new information about the red-ink warning with an accompanying sketch of the card and its clutching hand. The article ended with the words **'When will the fiend strike again?'**

"Scarlet Phantom indeed!" Seaton snorted. "What utter poppycock! I suppose you have also leaked to the press that you expect another visitation from this unseen villain tonight."

"Not at all, sir," McCorkle said patiently. "In fact, if I had been aware in advance of the threat delivered to Mr

Kincaid, I would have advised him not to share it with the press."

"I have made it clear that I require the utmost discretion." Seaton wagged a scolding finger. "I cannot allow myself or my business to become the object of such lurid sensationalism."

"I'm sure no one wants that, sir," McCorkle assured him.

Seaton snatched the newspaper back from the constable and scowled at the headline before tossing it aside. "All this fuss over a bandit whose existence is quite impossible. Your being here at all is an utter waste of time."

"Now, now, sir," said the inspector, "if the evening passes without incident, all well and good. But if the criminal should strike, I believe you will be very grateful to have the police on hand."

"I intend to work alone in my study." Seaton pointed to a door at the far end of the parlour. "I shall be dealing with a number of confidential documents and I can't have strangers looking over my shoulder while I conduct my business."

"I assure you, sir, that we would do no such thing," said McCorkle.

"Why should I trust you?" Seaton demanded. He swept a hostile gaze over all of them. "Any of you? In fact, any one of you might be this fiend. The whole thing might be a hocus cooked up by the police to glorify themselves."

Artie found it curious that the man kept changing his mind. One moment the Phantom couldn't possibly exist, the next moment it might be any one of them who was bent on robbing him. He thought it best to say nothing.

"Surely you cannot suppose—" McCorkle began.

"You and your associates may post yourselves out here," the merchant snapped. "I shall lock myself in the study and work on my private papers – alone. Simpkin!" He caught the eye of his pale secretary. "Bring me a decanter of brandy."

"Immediately, sir." Simpkin bobbed his head and scurried off.

Seaton disappeared into the study, banging the door shut after him.

"Well, he isn't exactly grateful for our help, is he?" Pennycook noted wryly.

McCorkle scowled at the study door. "You will find, Constable, as you advance through the ranks, that a policeman is rarely welcomed warmly, even by those he seeks to protect."

"What do you expect to happen tonight, Inspector?" Artie asked.

"I have no idea," McCorkle replied, rubbing his moustache. "I intend to place myself by the door so that no robber, invisible or otherwise, can possibly get by me."

"Is there any other way into the study?" Pennycook inquired.

McCorkle shook his head. "I inspected the room thoroughly. There is only this door, and the window is securely fastened from the inside. There is a fireplace, but the chimney is too narrow to admit even a small child."

"I expect we're in for a dull night of it then," the constable concluded.

He could not have been more wrong.

6.

The Phantom Strikes

Artie, McCorkle and Pennycook settled themselves onto three hard, straight-backed chairs and began their vigil in the parlour of the merchant's grand town house. When Simpkin appeared with his master's brandy, he was so hunched over and silent, Artie barely noticed him until he was at the study door. He tapped lightly and was summoned into the room by a barked command. When he reappeared, he made a final grovelling bow before closing the door.

Turning to the three visitors, he said, "Might I offer you gentlemen some coffee?"

"Good idea," said the inspector. "It will help us to stay alert."

"If there's anything to stay alert for," Constable Pennycook murmured.

A few minutes later the secretary arrived with a pot of coffee. He poured three cups and left, saying he would be in his upstairs bedroom if anything else was required.

"What a strange little fellow he is," commented McCorkle, picking up his cup.

The next two hours passed uneventfully. Artie was glad he had brought a book to read – *Rob Roy* by Sir Walter Scott, which told of the adventures of a bold Scottish outlaw. The exciting tale helped him ignore how uncomfortable his chair was.

Inspector McCorkle occupied himself with reading every word in the newspaper and occasionally closing his eyes for a brief nap. Constable Pennycook periodically got up to pace the floor then sat down again with his gaze moving back and forth between the study door and the door that led out into the hallway.

When the grandfather clock in the corner struck half past nine, it roused McCorkle from a light slumber. His eye roved around the room, then briefly back to the paper before alighting upon Pennycook, who was alternately chewing the end of a pencil and scribbling in a notepad. "What are you scrawling there, Constable?"

Pennycook completed a sentence before looking up. "Making a few notes, sir, you know, to sharpen my detective skills."

"And what skills would those be exactly?" McCorkle was clearly amused.

Pennycook's eyed kindled with enthusiasm. "I am

studying the methods of C. Auguste Dupin."

"And who might he be?" the inspector inquired. "A French gentleman I assume."

"He is a character in the stories of the American writer Edgar Allan Poe, sir, featuring most notably in his mystery tale 'The Murders in the Rue Morgue'."

Artie recognised the name at once. He had read some of Mr Poe's chilling and atmospheric stories.

McCorkle eyed the constable indulgently. "I don't see what stories have to do with police work."

"Ah, well, sir, Monsieur Dupin has developed a most interesting technique for reading people's thoughts simply by studying them."

"Sounds like a parlour trick to me," scoffed the inspector.

"I assure you, sir, it is extremely scientific."

Artie almost groaned at hearing Peril's favourite word coming from the lips of the young policeman.

"Dupin demonstrates the technique upon a friend of his by observing the movements of his eyes and his facial expressions," Pennycook continued.

"And I suppose you can demonstrate this little trick on me, can you?" challenged the inspector.

"That's exactly what I have been doing, sir. No disrespect intended, of course."

McCorkle was sceptical but intrigued. "Go on then – what have I been thinking about?"

54

Pennycook tapped the pencil against his chin. "I should say you are thinking of buying a new carpet."

"Really?" McCorkle's eyebrows almost disappeared under the brim of his hat. "And what leads you to that conclusion?"

"It's very simple, sir," the constable explained. "I saw you stare at the carpet, then at the advertisements for household goods in the paper, then you frowned in thought. Clearly you noticed this fine carpet, spotted an advert for new carpets in the paper and pondered whether or not to buy one for yourself."

Artie was impressed. "Why, that's very clever, Constable."

McCorkle, however, gave a hearty laugh. "You and your friend Monsieur Dupin are barking up the wrong tree there, Pennycook. I spotted a wine stain on the carpet and wondered why it hadn't been cleaned up. My wife has been demanding a night out, so I looked in the paper to see what acts are performing at the Regency Theatre in the coming week. Then I was thinking to myself that I would like more coffee if we could rustle some up."

Sheepishly, Pennycook closed his notepad and put his pencil back in his pocket. "Well, the method's not perfect, but it could prove useful to the policemen of the future."

"Until that day comes," said McCorkle, "we shall have

to stick to the tried-and-true methods of investigation without any help from Monsieur Dupin."

Artie was glad he wasn't the only one who thought there were things to learn from stories. However, the ideas outlined by Mr Poe were clearly more complex than Pennycook imagined.

The inspector yawned and stretched his arms above his head. "Not much longer now and we can all go home," he said with one eye on the clock.

Artie was also watching the time go by, and the nearer they drew to the ten o'clock deadline mentioned in the note, the more certain he felt that something would happen. His ears were alert for every sound: the fateful ticking of the clock, the faint rustling of the wind in the trees outside, the grunts and sighs of his companions. He found it impossible to focus his attention on Sir Walter Scott's tale, his imagination completely absorbed in thoughts of the Scarlet Phantom.

When the hands on the clock worked their way around to ten o'clock, Artie was just beginning to wonder if perhaps Constable Pennycook was right after all when there came a sudden loud crash from the study.

"No! No! Leave me alone!" they heard Seaton cry out.

Leaping from their chairs, McCorkle and Pennycook bounded for the door, with Artie right behind them. The inspector yanked at the doorknob and growled in frustration.

"He's locked it, just as he said he would – the fool!"

"Help! Help!" came Seaton's voice. It was cut off in a strangled screech of pain.

McCorkle threw his shoulder against the door but to no avail.

"Perhaps the two of us, sir," Pennycook suggested.

Artie dodged aside as the two policemen took a few steps back, then charged at the same time. This time there was a definite splintering of wood. At their second charge, the lock broke off and the door flew wide open.

Carried on by their own momentum, the two policemen staggered into the room. Following hard on their heels, Artie saw Seaton slumped on the floor against the far wall, groaning and clutching his head. Papers from his desk were strewn across the floor and at his feet lay a small bronze bust of the Duke of Wellington.

To the merchant's left, his wall safe gaped open.

McCorkle bent over the victim. "Who was it?" he demanded loudly. "What happened to you, sir?"

"Attacked," Seaton answered feebly. "Couldn't see him."

"There must be some way in," Constable Pennycook muttered, running his hand over the wall. "A secret door or suchlike."

Artie decided to check on a more obvious entrance. He rushed to the window and pulled the curtains aside.

57

It was closed and snibbed on the inside, with no sign of a forced entry. Suddenly a flicker of movement beyond the glass pane caught his eye.

"Inspector!" he yelled. "There's somebody outside the window!"

7.

The Lurking Shadow

Before Inspector McCorkle could respond to Artie, Seaton grabbed him by the lapel and pulled him close.

"Help me! Help me!" he croaked.

Constable Pennycook, with one hand still feeling for cracks in the wall, glanced in the direction of the window. "I can't see anything."

"I tell you there's someone out there!" exclaimed Artie. He made a dash for the open doorway. "We mustn't let him get away!"

Racing into the parlour, he collided with Simpkin and both of them tumbled to the floor.

"Oh, dear, dear, whatever is happening?" the timid secretary squeaked. Artie disentangled himself and scrambled to his feet. Leaving Simpkin still gasping on the floor, he bolted for the front door. Once outside, he raced round the corner of the house to the lawn and flower beds overlooked by the study window.

In the gloom of night, he saw a dark figure flitting through the trees towards the high garden wall. Charging after it, Artie yelled, "Halt there! Halt in the name of the law!"

As soon as the words were out of his mouth they sounded utterly foolish to his own ears. He was not the law, and even if he were, it seemed unlikely that the fleeing stranger would stop on the command of a boy.

Skirting a flower bed, the shadow took a run at the wall and swarmed over it, as nimble as a cat. Pelting after it, Artie made a jump of his own, but his grip fell short and he slid down onto the grass with a grunt of frustration. He looked around to see if there was a handy tree he could climb to get himself over. Before he could pick one out, he was hailed by the voice of Constable Pennycook.

"Hey there, don't you move!"

Artie caught the glare of the policeman's lantern directly in his eyes. Pennycook advanced quickly and exclaimed, "Why, young Mr Doyle! That was rather a rash thing to do, dashing off like that."

"Whoever it was got away," Artie grumbled. "If Simpkin hadn't got in my way, I might have caught up with him."

Pennycook stared at him quizzically. "Are you quite sure you saw someone at the window? It was very dark."

"I'm perfectly sure," Artie insisted. "I saw him escape over the wall."

"Tell you what," the constable suggested, "let's go have a look over there by the window. Perhaps your shadow left some traces behind."

Retracing their steps to the side of the house, they saw that the study curtains were once again closed. The constable shone his lantern over the ground beneath the window and peered closely.

"No sign of any footprints," he noted. "Mind you, the turf is quite springy."

Bending down, Artie felt around in the grass, hoping to discover some clue, a dropped button or a cigarette end. Disappointingly all he found were a few thin flakes of wood.

"What's that you've got there?" the constable wondered, shining his lantern on the tiny slivers in Artie's palm. "That won't be much help."

"No, I don't suppose it will," Artie sighed. Nevertheless, he wrapped the wood flakes in a page torn from his notebook and slipped them into his pocket.

"We'd best get back inside," Pennycook advised. "The inspector will be wondering what's become of us."

When they returned to the study, Artie saw that Seaton was now seated in a leather chair, mopping his brow with a silk kerchief. In his other hand he held a glass of brandy from which he took the occasional noisy sip. Simpkin stood by with the decanter, ready to refill his master's glass as soon as it was empty. The secretary had turned so pale, Artie thought he could be mistaken for a ghost in a stage play.

While Constable Pennycook resumed his search for secret panels in the walls, the inspector finished writing down the victim's account of his ordeal.

Flicking through his notes, he said, "Now, Mr Seaton, let's make sure I've got this right. You were seated at your desk when you felt yourself seized from behind. You were hurled over the desk, so scattering these papers we see lying about. When you got up from the floor, you observed this bronze bust of the late Duke of Wellington flying through the air towards you."

The inspector nodded towards the statuette standing on the desktop. "It struck you on the side of the head, so that you fell back against the wall and lay stunned on the floor for perhaps half a minute."

"That is correct," said Seaton, gingerly fingering the left side of his head.

Artie noticed a streak of blood in the man's white hair. Picking up the bust, he turned it over and spotted a crimson smear on the base. This seemed to confirm the merchant's story.

McCorkle also noticed the blood. "Would you like us to send for a doctor, sir?"

"No," snapped Seaton, "I want you to get my rubies back. How the fiend managed to open the safe is beyond me."

Pennycook lifted up the edge of the Persian rug to look for a trapdoor.

Artie thought for a moment, trying to calculate any way the theft might have been carried out. What if the blow on the head had confused Seaton and he was mistaken about the rubies? "Are you sure the jewels were there in the first place?" he asked hesitantly.

"Why, you impertinent whelp!" Seaton snapped. "The inspector here saw me put them inside the safe. He even examined them."

"Correct, sir, quite correct," McCorkle confirmed, hoping to pacify the merchant. "And I saw you lock it securely."

Constable Pennycook scanned the ceiling, but there was no means of entry or exit up there. "The villain appears to be even more resourceful than his first robbery demonstrated," he observed. "Not only can he render himself unseen, but he now seems able to walk through locked doors and to disappear at will."

Artie realised that the two policemen were staring at him, as though they expected him to come up with some brilliant idea.

"Well, McCorkle, what do you intend to do about this outrage?" Seaton demanded.

The inspector gave his moustache an irritated tug. "We shall apply all the resources at our command to find a solution to this most vexing mystery."

"Your performance tonight does not fill me with confidence," the merchant retorted sourly. "Perhaps you can come up with a more intelligent plan than recruiting children to do your work for you."

McCorkle winced as though he had been jabbed with a needle. "Yes, well, we had best get back to the office and make out a report." He added in a low murmur, "Not that anyone's going to believe it."

They left Seaton to the care of his timorous secretary. It was a relief to get out into the fresh night air and away from the irritable textile merchant. Artie wondered if it was the Phantom he had spotted fleeing across the garden. But if the thief was able to pass through the walls of the house in order to steal the rubies, why would he need to climb over the garden wall?

"Constable Pennycook, go and fetch us a cab," the inspector instructed. "We'll drop our young friend off at home on the way."

When the young policeman hurried out into the street, McCorkle addressed Artie gravely. "Mr Doyle, I must confess myself disappointed."

"Disappointed?" Artie echoed.

McCorkle gave a grim nod. "I had hoped you would provide some insights into this affair, but you seem just as baffled as I am. Until we make a breakthrough, I must ask you to keep tonight's events strictly confidential, and in particular do not share them with your parents."

Artie nodded. "Inspector, I promise you, I shall get to the bottom of this business."

But even as he spoke he felt a sinking sensation in his stomach. In his imagination, he saw the shadowy figure of the Phantom sneering at him and could almost hear the fiend's mocking laughter.

8.

Facts Not Fancies

When he got home, Artie found his mother waiting anxiously for him while his father was occupied in the back room finishing his latest painting, a ruined castle bathed in moonlight with some wild geese flying past the stars in the background. Following the inspector's instructions, he assured them both that absolutely nothing had happened at Seaton's house.

"There, I knew it was all nonsense," Mrs Doyle declared. "Probably a piece of tomfoolery created for the sake of gossip."

Artie was relieved that she accepted his story of a boring, uneventful vigil so easily. If he told her the truth, she'd very likely lead a whole regiment of priests down to Mr Seaton's house to do battle with the powers of darkness.

Before going to sleep, he tried to clarify his thoughts by writing down some notes:

The Phantom
- Invisible
- Walks through walls
- Throws things
- Opens safe
- Steals jewels

Artie tried to make sense of the Phantom's bizarre abilities, but his words began to swim about before his eyes and he drifted into sleep.

In the morning Artie hurried through his breakfast, then dashed off to find Ham. He arrived at his friend's house to find him struggling out the door with his huge black dog, Berrybus.

"Artie, thank goodness you're here. Can you give me a hand with him? He's being very lively this morning."

Berrybus reared up on his hind legs and, with his huge front paws, pinned Artie's shoulders against the wall. He then proceeded to lick his whole face with his long, wet tongue. When the dog finally dropped to the ground, Artie wiped his nose and cheeks with his sleeve.

"Ham, we need to go to Peril's house," he said.

"What for?" Ham asked as they manoeuvred the great hound out into the street. "To look at rocks?"

"There have been some developments in the case and I'm stumped. Peril's ideas so far haven't panned out, but she is good at coming up with theories."

"We're not going to have her trailing around after us like that other girl, are we?" Ham made a face like he had just been forced to swallow cod liver oil.

"If you're talking about Rowena," said Artie, "we'd have been in a real fix without her help."

The talents of the young actress Rowena McCleary had played an important role in their capture of the villain behind the mysterious case of the Vanishing Dragon last year.

"I say, you don't suppose she's back in town for the summer, do you?" Ham wondered.

"If she is," said Artie, "she's probably busy with her theatrical career."

"Fine!" said Ham with relief. "We can do without her. So what are these developments you were talking about?"

"I'll tell you all about it when we get to Peril's house. And I'm not sure we should bring Berrybus with us."

"We don't have any choice," said Ham. "The only way I could get out of practising piano all morning was to offer to take him for his walk." Ham's mother was a piano teacher and had musical ambitions for her son that went far beyond any signs of talent on his part.

Once they were out on the street, Ham had such a struggle controlling the immense hound, he hadn't enough breath left to ask questions. Artie took the card Peril had given him from his pocket and read it again:

Mrs Beatrice Carlyle Abernethy

GEOLOGIST

21B NEWINGTON PLACE
EDINBURGH

Once the dog had been treated to an energetic romp in the Meadows, the boys made their way to Newington Place, their progress hampered by Berrybus's insistence on stopping to investigate every new smell. Peril's home was an impressive two-storey townhouse with large bay windows. She herself answered the jangle of the door pull and ushered them inside.

"So you're here at last," she greeted them. "I wondered when you'd turn up. And where did you find that enormous beast? Why, he's positively prehistoric."

Berrybus wagged his heavy tail enthusiastically.

"This is my dog, Berrybus," said Ham. "He sometimes helps out on our cases."

"In a manner of speaking," added Artie. Their attempts to use Berrybus as a bloodhound last year to sniff out the trail of a criminal had met with mixed results.

"You're certainly a handsome fellow," Peril told the dog. "Show me how clever you are. Sit!"

To Artie's astonishment, the big dog obediently sank down on his haunches.

"Good boy!" said Peril approvingly. "Now give me a paw."

She held out her hand. Berrybus obligingly raised his left forefoot and placed it in her palm.

"I don't understand this at all." Ham was aghast. "I've been trying to train him all year and I can't get him to do anything."

Peril let the dog's paw drop and smiled at the boys. "He's actually rather dear, isn't he?"

"Yes, he's a friendly old soul," said Ham. "But I've never seen him do tricks before."

"Come on," said Peril, leading them through a door.

The room beyond was large and airy with a window overlooking a walled garden. There was a desk of black walnut with papers and magazines arranged neatly upon it, as well as pens, bottles of ink and several notepads. A tall bookcase crammed with textbooks occupied the adjacent wall. Artie noticed that one shelf was filled with the novels of the French author Jules Verne, such as *Journey to the Centre of the Earth* and *Five Weeks in a Balloon.*

Dominating the other side of the room was a large table on which were set out a microscope, a Bunsen burner and an array of test tubes and specimen cases. From the mantle above the fireplace, a small stuffed crocodile and a lamprey in a jar peered down at them.

They sat themselves around the desk while Berrybus plumped himself down on the carpet at Peril's feet.

"The Phantom struck again last night," Artie told the others, "and I'm afraid, Peril, that none of what happened will fit your theories."

"Never mind about that, Doyle," said Peril dismissively. "Let's hear your report."

Artie gave a full account of last night's events, including the inspector's instructions that they were to keep this information to themselves.

When he had finished his astonishing tale, Peril pushed her spectacles up to the bridge of her nose and gazed sternly at Artie like a teacher listening to a lame excuse for some missing homework.

"Let me make sure I understand you, Doyle," she said at last. "You're saying some invisible entity drifted past a police guard into a locked room, assaulted the occupant, removed jewels from a secure safe, then disappeared into thin air?"

Artie nodded unhappily. He was only too aware of how preposterous it all sounded. "It rather seems to defy explanation," he confessed.

"I suppose you think it was some sort of *miracle*," said Peril, pronouncing the word as though it had a sour taste.

"Not at all," said Artie. "Miracles come from God, and God doesn't help people commit robberies."

"No, I don't suppose he would," said Peril. She bit her lip and pondered a moment. "Let's approach this scientifically. The way we see things is when light reflects from an object and strikes the eye. To avoid being seen, you would have to alter light itself, which is a bit of a tall order."

"Perhaps the Phantom drinks some sort of chemical that makes him like glass," Artie offered, "you know, so that light passes through him."

"Wouldn't his clothes still be visible?" Ham wondered.

"Yes," Artie conceded, "I suppose he'd have to go around without any... well, you know."

Ham shuddered. "I certainly wouldn't fancy walking around windy Edinburgh without any clothes on. Brrrrrr!"

"Listen, you two," Peril interposed firmly, "we need facts not fancies. This imaginary and quite impossible potion of yours would most likely poison him. And for another thing, if light passed straight through him, he wouldn't be able to see. Not an ideal condition for a robber."

"Oh, I suppose you have some clever scientific

explanation," Artie challenged.

Goaded, Peril stood up and strode over to the bookcase. She ran her finger over some of the titles, then spun round. "Perhaps…" She raised her index finger in the air. "Perhaps he wears a suit made of mirrors that reflects light away from him."

"In that case, anyone looking at him would see their own reflection," said Artie, "and nobody saw that."

"Yes, yes, it was just an idea," said Peril irritably. She began pacing the room so quickly Artie had to twist his head back and forth to keep track of her.

"I hate to point this out," said Ham slowly, "but both of you are ignoring the most obvious explanation."

"Really, Hamilton?" Peril halted in front of him and crossed her arms. "And what would that be?"

"That he's a ghost," Ham declared. "Obviously."

"That would explain quite a bit," Artie acknowledged. "But ghosts don't go around stealing things, do they?"

"They might," said Ham. "A ghost might well get a bee in his bonnet about jewels. Maybe he was very poor when he was alive and he won't be allowed to enter Heaven until he makes himself rich."

Peril clutched her head and groaned. "The pair of you are being ridiculous! There are no such things as ghosts."

"You're sure of that, are you?" Artie countered. "Lots of people have seen them."

"Lots of people *say* they've seen them," Peril insisted. "Probably just a shadow or a trick of the light."

Ham confronted her squarely. "So if the Phantom isn't a ghost, how is he able to move about without being seen, walk through walls, send bronze busts flying through the air, and disappear without a trace?"

Peril huffed for several seconds, then muttered, "I don't know. Not yet." She stalked away, grumbling to herself. "Ghosts indeed!"

"To be honest, Ham," said Artie, "while I'm prepared to believe in ghosts, I've never heard of one behaving like this. Especially not delivering warnings beforehand."

"It's still the only way to explain it," Ham persisted.

"No, it's not." Peril rounded on the two boys. "Have either of you ever been to a magic show?"

"We actually know quite a bit about magic shows," said Artie.

"Well, those fellows make it look like they're doing the most impossible things," Peril continued, "but really it's all done with mirrors, smoke, dummies and suchlike. Pure trickery."

"Perhaps the police should just round up all the conjurers they can find and keep them locked up until one of them confesses," Ham suggested.

Peril snorted. "Don't be absurd."

"So, if it is a trick," said Artie, "how is it being done, who is doing it and why?"

Peril took off her spectacles and polished them with a soft cloth. "Most likely it's someone on the inside who would have the opportunity to rig up something like this."

"And who might that be?" Ham asked.

"What about this Simpkin?" Peril replaced her glasses. "The secretary you told us about?"

"Simpkin?" Artie said. "He's as timid as a mouse. I can't see him carrying out a jewel robbery."

"That could just be an act," Peril pointed out. "Since he lives and works in the house, he would have the opportunity to rig up some hidden mechanism that might buffet his employer with blasts of air or even some form of magnetism."

"Constable Pennycook made a thorough search for secret doors," Artie reminded her. "I think if there had been any sort of hidden device he would have stumbled upon it."

"Don't be so sure," said Peril. "He's just a plodding policeman after all and probably wouldn't notice any sort of clue. Really, this villain must have left some trace behind."

"Well, I did find these." Artie reached into his pocket and took out a folded piece of paper, which he opened to display the tiny shavings of wood.

"Those are just splinters of wood," said Ham. "What have they got to do with the Phantom?"

"I found them under the study window," Artie explained, "where I spotted that shadowy figure lurking."

To Artie's surprise, Peril took an immediate interest in his minor piece of evidence. "Let me see," she said, taking the paper from him and laying it on her desk. She whisked out her magnifying glass and made a minute examination.

"They're probably left from when the gardener was trimming the trees," said Ham.

"This wood doesn't come from a tree," Peril corrected him. "There are tiny flecks of red paint on it."

"Paint?" echoed Artie. "Why would there be paint?"

"Does that make a difference?" inquired Ham.

"Yes, yes, I see it now," Peril mused. "Do you know what these are? They are shavings from a pencil, cut off with a penknife."

"You mean somebody was standing at the window sharpening a pencil?" Ham was dubious. "Who on earth would do that?"

Artie clapped a hand to his forehead. "I know who!" he exclaimed. "It was the Ferret."

9.

On the Trail of the Ferret

The next instant, Peril's house was rocked by a loud bang. Startled, Berrybus leapt to his feet, howling in dismay.

"Oh no, not again!" Peril groaned, heading for the door.

While Ham struggled to calm the huge black dog, Artie followed the girl up the hallway to the source of the noise. A door was flung open before them with a sign on it that read:

KNOCK BEFORE
ENTERING

A gust of acrid smoke wafted out, followed by a handsome woman wearing goggles and a smock stained with chemicals. She closed the door behind her and all three of them spent a few moments coughing as the fumes dissipated.

"Mother!" Peril scolded once the air had cleared. "You promised!"

"Yes, I know," the woman responded. "I was not expecting the solution to prove so volatile. But look at the result."

She handed her daughter what looked like half of a rock that had been split sharply down the middle. Peril adjusted her glasses and peered.

"Why, it's some sort of trilobite!"

"Yes, which confirms my theory that the whole area will prove a rich source of fresh fossils." The woman turned abruptly and thrust her hand at Artie. "Young man, I do not believe I have had the pleasure. Beatrice Abernethy."

In spite of the fact that her hand was peppered with black powder, Artie shook it politely. "Arthur Conan Doyle, ma'm," he introduced himself.

Beatrice Abernethy tapped the rock with one finger. "Were you aware, young man, that Edinburgh is the birthplace of geology? Oh yes, it was while examining the Salisbury Crags out by Arthur's Seat that the great James Hutton first formulated his theory that igneous rock has a volcanic origin far older than any biblical calendar."

Before Artie could respond, an enthusiastic panting announced the arrival of Berrybus. Dragging Ham helplessly along at the other end of his lead, the great hound made straight for Mrs Abernethy. He reared up, planting his enormous paws on her shoulders.

Beatrice Abernethy calmly raised her goggles and scrutinised the dog with her intelligent blue eyes. "Ah, a mastiff – a very stalwart breed, descended from the ancient Alaunt and the *Pugnaces Britanniae*."

Berrybus rewarded her tribute with a lick on her nose before dropping down to lope back to his master.

Ham was impressed. "You know a lot about dogs."

"I know a lot about every animal," said Beatrice Abernethy. "That, combined with my expertise in geology, makes me one of the leading figures in the new science of *palaeontology*."

The last word rolled slowly off her tongue as though she relished the sound of it. Smiling at her daughter, she observed, "So, Pearl, are these the interesting young men you were telling me about – the investigators?"

Artie nodded and Ham introduced himself. "Edward Hamilton, miss, I mean ma'm."

"Beatrice Abernethy," said the woman, shaking him by the hand.

"Whenever there's any funny business going on," Ham continued, "you'll find us there. Not that we cause the funny business, you understand," he added hastily.

"Indeed, it is by investigating puzzles and anomalies

that we make new discoveries," said Beatrice Abernethy approvingly, "and achieve important breakthroughs in our understanding of the world. Just like when we pry open an oyster to find the precious pearl inside."

She gave her daughter an affectionate sidelong glance as she said 'pearl'.

"You mean like the precious stone?" Ham was momentarily confused. "But she told us her name was spelled like – urk!"

He cried out as Peril stamped on his foot to silence him. "Hamilton, the kitchen is through that green door," she suggested pointedly. "Why don't you take your dog in there and give him a bowl of water to drink?"

"I suppose he could probably do with a drink," Ham conceded. As he dragged Berrybus away, he mumbled, "No need to stamp on a chap's foot…"

Beatrice Abernethy took a cloth from a pocket of her smock and began to wipe the soot marks from her face. Surveying Artie and Peril, she asked, "So, are you any closer to clearing up this Phantom nonsense?"

"I have just discovered a clue," said Peril with a glow of satisfaction.

"And we'd better follow it up right away," Artie put in, "while the trail is still fresh." He didn't want Peril repeating his account of last night's events until they had made some progress.

"I quite understand," said the lady geologist, replacing her goggles. "I must continue with my work also. It was a pleasure to meet you, Mr Doyle, and your friend Mr Hamilton." As she headed back into the smoky laboratory she paused to ask, "What is the name of his splendid dog?"

"Berrybus."

"Yes, very fitting. Don't be late for tea again, Pearl. We need to plan our trip to the Botanic Gardens on Saturday."

The door closed and Peril tutted to herself. "I do worry about her."

"She strikes me as a very competent lady," Artie commented honestly.

"Yes, of course, she is but… Look, we'd best get going. Where is Hamilton?"

"Here," said Ham, emerging from the kitchen with Berrybus, whose muzzle was dripping with water. "All I could find was a bucket, but that seemed to suit him."

As they walked up the hallway, Peril ducked back into her study to fetch her equipment.

"I'd better get Berrybus back home," said Ham as he and Artie stepped outside. "He's getting hungry and I don't want him to eat some passing cat."

"He certainly seems to have taken a liking to Peril and her mother," said Artie.

"You'd almost think he knew they were named after a biscuit," said Ham.

"Look, Peril and I will go and have a talk with the Ferret. We'll catch up with you later."

"Alright," Ham agreed. He added in a warning tone, "Don't let her blow you up or anything."

As he disappeared up the street, being dragged helplessly along, Peril joined Artie on the doorstep. He explained that Ham was going home and the two of them set off for town.

"My mother, as you can see, is a very intelligent and practical woman," said Peril. "She'll have no truck with ghosts and goblins, and neither will I."

"And we're interesting young men, eh?" said Artie. "I didn't know you thought so highly of us."

"I don't," said Peril tartly. "But I could hardly tell my mother I was associating with a pair of rash buffoons whose heads are full of wild fancies, could I?"

"No, I don't suppose you could," said Artie, trying not to sound insulted. "So was your father not at home today?"

"No." A shadow passed over Peril's face and she thrust her hands into her pockets. "The fact is, Doyle... The fact is that he died last year. A rockfall in the Pyrenees."

Artie felt his stomach sink. Many times over the past few years he had feared losing his own father to ill health. "Oh, I'm sorry to hear that. It must have been dreadful. Ham's had to get along without his father too, and I know it isn't easy."

"He was Dr Richard Abernethy, the eminent geologist," said Peril, her sadness tinged with pride. "If he had lived he would have become famous for the discoveries he would have made. That's why mother and I are so intent on searching for fossils."

"I don't understand."

Peril stopped and they faced each other. In her eye was the tiniest gleam of an unshed tear. "We want to discover the remains of some prehistoric creature that no one has found before. Then we'll name it after my father in his honour. It will be called something like *Neosaurus richardensis*."

"I'm sure that will be a very fine tribute."

Peril sighed. "I only hope we can succeed."

"I think anything's possible," said Artie, "for a girl whose name means danger."

Although she tried to hide it, Artie spotted a pleased smile on Peril's face before she turned away at the sound of a news vendor peddling his wares on the corner.

"The Phantom strikes again! Read all about it here!"

Artie was taken aback to hear that the robbery had made the news when Inspector McCorkle had been so determined to keep the incident under wraps. He felt around in his pocket for change and bought a copy of the *Scotsman*. He and Peril pressed together as they scanned the story with eager eyes.

THE PHANTOM STRIKES AGAIN!

◆

The Scarlet Phantom, the invisible fiend who has already terrorised George Street with his bold assault on Mr Royston Kincaid on Monday morning, has attacked again, mysteriously penetrating the locked study of another of Edinburgh's leading citizens.

The story continued in this rather purple style, but Artie noticed that it was very short on details. The only facts presented were that a warning had been left for Mr Seaton and that, despite a police guard, he had been attacked in his study. There was nothing about the safe or the stolen rubies.

"This seems to confirm that the Ferret was hiding outside the study window," Artie surmised.

"Might he be the one who engineered those events?" Peril wondered. "He might have obtained some sort of device that could penetrate the room and thrust Seaton against the wall."

"Even supposing he had such a thing," Artie objected, "why on earth would he do it?"

"To create a sensational story that will bring him fame,"

said Peril. "That's what every journalist wants, isn't it?"

"I'm not convinced," said Artie, "but let's find out what he has to say for himself."

The *Scotsman* offices were halfway down Cockburn Street. As soon as they walked through the front doors, Artie and Peril found themselves almost overwhelmed by the clatter and bustle. From under their feet came the clanking and pounding of the great printing machines rolling off fresh copies of the *Scotsman.* Men in ink-stained aprons rushed to and fro with sheaves of paper and wooden boxes under their arms. Boys in ragged caps bolted in and out of the many doors waving messages in the air.

Artie hooked one of the newsboys by the arm to inquire where he might find Mr Ferryman. The boy answered with a tilt of the head towards the iron stairway and an upward jab of his thumb before wrenching free and disappearing into a cacophonous back room.

"This place is certainly busy," Peril commented approvingly as she and Artie climbed upwards.

The metal steps rang like discordant bells beneath the feet of men and boys charging up and down on their fevered business.

"For all the attention anybody's paying us," said Artie, "*we* might as well be invisible."

On the upper floor they saw an array of desks set at

haphazard angles to each other where journalists were writing up their stories. All across the room loud voices demanded more ink, more paper and lots of strong black tea. Artie spotted Ferryman leaning back in his desk chair, his eyes fixed at some point on the ceiling while he whittled at a pencil, paying no attention to the wood shavings dropping to the floor at his feet.

Though he appeared distracted, Artie and Peril had no sooner started towards him than his small sharp eyes fixed upon them. A sly smirk twisted the thin lips beneath his ginger moustache.

"Ah, I was wondering when you'd turn up."

10.

The Crimes of Cadwallader Figg

"You were expecting us?" Artie was quite taken aback by Ferryman's greeting.

"Oh, I anticipated you'd come and try to pick my brains, Mr... Doyle, is it?"

"Yes, and this is Miss Abernethy."

"Scientific investigator," Peril added stiffly.

"Heard old McCorkle had brought you in on this case," said the Ferret, "a bit like a private bloodhound. Heard he brought you to Seaton's house last night to watch out for the Phantom."

"Where you had concealed yourself in the garden," said Peril. "But to what purpose?" she added accusingly.

"To get a story of course," Ferryman chortled. "From outside I couldn't pick up much beyond some uproar in the study." He flipped open his notebook and poised his freshly sharpened pencil over the page. "How about a few details, Mr Doyle? The public does have a right to know."

"How did you even know the Phantom had threatened Mr Seaton?" Artie demanded. "That wasn't made public."

"Got my sources inside the Police Office," said the Ferret, knowingly touching his nose. "A constable or two ready to share information with an old mate like me, so long as there's a bottle of whisky in it."

"That hardly sounds very ethical," said Peril sternly.

"It's business, my girl, business," said the reporter airily. "One hand scratches the other, so to speak. We might do that now, Mr Doyle. I can offer an exchange of information."

"It sounds like I have more information than you," said Artie cautiously. "Why should I share any of it?"

Ferryman leaned forward and winked. "Because for all that, you have no clue as to the identity of the Scarlet Phantom."

"And just where exactly did the name the Scarlet Phantom come from?" Peril adjusted her spectacles and glared suspiciously at the reporter.

"Dreamed it up myself," Ferryman admitted proudly. "Makes a good headline, eh?"

"But are you claiming you have a clue to his identity?" said Artie.

Ferryman sat back in his chair and twirled the pencil back and forth across his fingers, like a juggler showing off a trick. "Twelve years tramping around the streets of Edinburgh with my eyes and ears wide open has given me access to a treasury of invaluable information. Every alleyway, every back room, every unsolved crime, every pickpocket and burglar that ever climbed through an unlocked window – got them all here." He tapped himself on the head with the end of the pencil. "If the police knew half as much as I do, they'd be twice as effective."

"So you're saying that you're on the trail of the invisible robber," said Artie.

"I'm saying I know where the trail begins," said Ferryman smugly. "But as for where it ends…" – he tossed the pencil in the air and caught it nimbly – "that's another matter."

"So you want to trade information," said Peril. "Some of the facts in our possession in exchange for…?"

"The trail of the Phantom," Ferryman concluded.

Artie and Peril exchanged questioning glances.

"Come on," Ferryman urged. "If you can't trust a journalist, who can you trust?"

Artie wasn't sure he could trust the Ferret, and he hadn't forgotten Peril's suspicions that the reporter had somehow engineered the two robberies himself in order to create a series of dramatic headlines. On the other hand, he couldn't pass up the chance to pick up the Phantom's trail, especially as he had no leads of his own.

"Alright, I can tell you this much," he began. "Mr Seaton was alone in his locked study with the police on guard on the other side of the door."

"I had worked out that much for myself," Ferryman grumbled.

"In spite of the fact that nobody else was in the room," Artie went on, "Seaton was violently handled and thrust against the wall."

Ferryman nodded, prompting him to continue.

"He was then struck on the head with a bust of the Duke of Wellington."

"Wellington, eh?" Ferryman's eyes lit up with excitement as he noted down the details. "That's a good touch. So this bust, it…?"

"Flew though the air and hit him. I saw blood on his hair and on the base of the statuette."

"Anything stolen?"

"Some rubies," Artie answered reluctantly. "And that's all I can tell you."

"That will do, that will do," said the Ferret, drumming on his desk with the pencil. "I can dress it up a bit for the evening paper."

"Now what about your part of the bargain?" said Peril. "You said you would put us on the trail of the Phantom.

Or was that just bluster?"

"No need to take that tone," Ferryman responded. "I didn't become Edinburgh's leading newsman without keeping my word. Come in closer."

Artie and Peril drew in until their faces were only inches from the point of his nose.

"Now, I think we can agree that these are the most astonishing crimes ever to terrorise this fair city. It's obvious that this Phantom is no common thief but someone of extraordinary abilities."

"So far, all you're doing is stating the obvious," said Peril.

"Now now, my girl, one step at a time," Ferryman chided her. "I'm just getting started."

Peril bridled at being addressed as 'my girl' again, but kept her mouth shut so that Ferryman might continue.

"That being the case," said the reporter, "it seems to me that there's only one man in Edinburgh, only one man in the whole country, with the resources and the genius to pull this off." His voice dropped to a husky whisper. "His name is Cadwallader Figg."

"Figg?" Artie shook his head. "I've never heard of him."

"Are you quite sure of that?" Ferret inquired meaningfully.

"It's not the sort of name anybody is liable to forget," Peril pointed out.

"Good," said Ferryman. "It's much safer that you don't know him."

"And why is that?" Artie was almost bristling with curiosity.

"He is the emperor of crime," the Ferret informed them darkly, "like a giant spider at the centre of an evil web. But he works through so many proxies, cat's paws and henchmen, it's impossible ever to pin anything on him."

"If he is such a villain," said Peril, "why don't you expose him in your newspaper?"

"Expose him?" Ferryman was shocked. "If we as much as mentioned his name in print, he'd have his lawyers all over us like a pack of starving wolves, and we have no proof of any of this. Oh no, I steer well clear of that gentleman. It's not unknown for persons who cross his path to simply disappear." He snapped his fingers to indicate how easily the great criminal made people vanish.

"But isn't the point of investigating these crimes to expose the culprit?" said Artie.

"That's the job of the police," Ferryman corrected him. "My job is to come up with a good story that will fill a few columns, and that's all the Scarlet Phantom is to me."

"So are the police pursuing this man Figg?" asked Peril.

"Pursuing him?" The Ferret's moustache twitched with amusement. "I should say not. I told you, he covers his tracks so well they couldn't pin as much as a stolen inkwell on him if they put every man on the case."

"Are they even aware of his existence?" Peril persisted.

"Oh yes, as a businessman, as an importer of tea and a dealer in antiques."

"So he does carry on legitimate business," said Artie.

"You may have heard of Sino-Britannic Imports or Imperial Antiquities Incorporated. All him." The Ferret gave Artie a knowing wink. "Now, Mr Doyle, if I was to investigate Figg, I would begin there. But my face is too well known. I'd be spotted right off. But if some kiddies were to have a nose around, why, they wouldn't be suspected at all."

"So what you're saying is—" Artie began.

"I'm saying nothing," Ferryman interrupted. "Mum's the word, remember. Now then, as to this business of the Duke of Wellington flying through the air – who actually witnessed the phenomenon?"

"I'm afraid I can't really tell you any more." Artie backed away, beckoning to Peril to join him.

"If you do come up with any useful tidbits," said the Ferret as he waved them goodbye, "be sure to let me know. I can make it worth your while. I have some sweets here in my desk."

"Sweets indeed!" humphed Peril as they walked down the metal stairs. "Imagine treating us as though we were children."

"He did give us a lead," Artie reminded her.

"What, this Cadwallader Figg person?" Peril scoffed. "Even if he exists – which I doubt – he's probably some harmless old miser."

Artie wasn't so sure. "I don't think we can just discount this information, Peril."

Peril shrugged. "You can waste your time chasing wild geese, if you like. I'd better go home and make sure Mother doesn't blow up anything valuable."

Later that day, after making one or two stops along the way, Artie returned to Ham's house to share the information he had gained from the Ferret. They retreated to the kitchen while in the front room one of Mrs Hamilton's unhappy piano pupils was doing ear-jangling violence to one of Chopin's waltzes.

Putting the kettle on, Ham cut some slices of bread and set out a pot of blackcurrant jam. While they fortified themselves with cups of tea and jam sandwiches, Artie brought Ham up to date with the investigation.

"So you think this Catwalloper Frog is the invisible fiend?" said Ham.

"Cadwallader Figg," Artie corrected him. "I don't know about that, but the Ferret is right that it would take somebody with a lot of ingenuity to pull off this kind of trick."

Ham took a swallow of tea. "You mean some kind of criminal mastermind? Honestly Artie, that sounds like something from one of those stories you read."

"It does sound extraordinary," Artie admitted.

Reaching for another slice of bread, Ham pondered the matter. "Look, I don't know about you, but I think Ferryman is sending you in the wrong direction so that you don't get in the way of his story." He spooned a liberal dollop of jam over the bread and fed a piece of crust to Berrybus, who was nestled around his feet.

"That may be true," Artie conceded, "but it's the only lead we've got." He opened his notebook and read aloud his fresh information:

On the way here I stopped off at the Post Office in Waterloo Place to consult the Edinburgh Business Directory. I found that both Sino-Britannic Imports and Imperial Antiquities Incorporated have premises in Leith.

Ham licked some jam from his fingers and stared at his friend. "Why did you do that, Artie?"

"Because," Artie answered in a determined voice, "if the Ferret is too scared to investigate Cadwallader Figg, we're not."

"Are you sure we're not?" Ham turned a little pale.

"Yes," Artie said firmly.

He took out his pencil and was about to add something to his notes when Ham stopped him.

"Artie, maybe you shouldn't write down anything about Figg, you know, just to be on the safe side."

Artie recalled the Ferret's warning about what happened to people who spread the master criminal's name about. "You're right, Ham. I'll keep that part of the case in my head."

Putting his notebook away, Artie rose decisively from the table. "Come on, Ham, we're going to find out all we can about this supposed emperor of crime."

Ham stared dolefully at his final slice of bread and jam. "I hope this doesn't turn out to be the condemned man's last meal."

11.

The Return of Beresford Root

The gulls that wheeled and cawed in the air overhead told the boys that they were now close to Leith Harbour, as did the salty tang gusting into the air from the sea. Storehouses, taverns and seamen's hostels rose up on either side of the narrow road where wagons squeezed past each other with their loads of coal, timber and bales of fabric.

"Artie, are you sure we should be doing this?" Ham complained. "Didn't the Ferret say that Cantankerous Fizz can make people disappear?"

"Cadwallader Figg," Artie corrected him. "He may not be so dangerous as Ferryman makes out. I think he likes to make things up for the sake of a good story, just like he invented the name the Scarlet Phantom for our invisible man."

"You know, Artie," said Ham thoughtfully, "there is one

thing we haven't considered. Maybe the invisible man is actually an invisible woman."

"A woman?" Artie was sceptical. "I don't think so, Ham."

"Why not? That Mrs Abernethy obviously knows a lot about science. Maybe she's found a way to make herself invisible and is stealing jewels in order to finance her fossil hunting."

"I don't know about that. She seems, well, too nice."

"That could just be an act to throw us off the track. And in that case, Peril is probably in on it too."

"Peril? But she's been helping with the investigation."

"Don't be fooled by that, Artie. Girls can be quite devious."

"Ham, just because she's clever doesn't mean you can't trust her," said Artie. "You're being ridiculous."

In the distance they could hear dock workers calling to each other as they unloaded fresh cargo from a newly arrived ship. The words of a raucous sea shanty wafted from an open tavern window, something about a woman named Nelly who lived in Shanghai.

"Over there," said Artie pointing, "that's what we're looking for."

A large building directly ahead bore a painted sign with the words:

SINO-BRITANNIC IMPORTS

Two muscular men with long black hair and dragon tattoos on their arms were carrying crates from a wagon into the front door.

"I don't think we want to mix with those two," Ham muttered. "They look dangerous."

Artie pointed to a narrow alley next to the building. "We'll go around the back," he said, leading the way.

Ham followed reluctantly. "Artie, this is a bit risky. What on earth do you expect to find in there?"

"Remember Professor Anderson's mechanical dragon?" Artie referred back to their last case. "It was built and stored in a building just like that. Now, if Peril is right and this is all being accomplished by some mechanical device, then this is just the sort of place to hide it."

At the rear of the building they found a door, which disappointed them by being securely locked. "Not to worry," said Artie, indicating a nearby window that lay partially ajar.

"It's a bit high," Ham noted.

"You'll just have to give me a boost," said Artie.

With a resigned huff, Ham offered his cupped hands and Artie placed his foot on them. Ham gave an upward heave which lifted his friend high enough to reach the window ledge and push it open. He scrambled up, then reached down to pull Ham up with him. Together they dropped to the floor in the dimly lit interior.

They found themselves in a maze of shelves piled high with wooden boxes and walls of stacked packing cases.

"I can't say it looks like anything mechanical has been built here," said Ham.

"Maybe not," Artie conceded, "but we should have a good look around. We might find some trace of the stolen jewels or even evidence of some of Figg's other crimes."

Slowly they made their way down the narrow passages between the shelves and the stacks of packing cases which blocked the light from the windows. The deeper they penetrated, the thicker grew the gloom until they could barely make out each other. A sudden scuffling noise put them on alert and they pressed together for protection.

"What was that?" Ham whispered.

Artie put a finger to his lips to hush his friend and they stood stock still, listening. It sounded like dragging footsteps drawing closer.

"I can hear somebody breathing," Ham gasped. "Artie, what if it's the Phantom?"

Artie shushed his friend and together they shrank back from the approaching presence. Artie felt a cold dread clutch at his heart and he struggled to fight down the terror rising up in his chest. Had they walked into a trap? Had the Scarlet Phantom been lying in wait for them all along?

At that moment a box dislodged itself from a shelf above them and crashed to the floor, smashing to pieces at their feet. Artie couldn't hold back a yelp of alarm.

"It's the Phantom!" Ham squealed. "He's trying to kill us!"

Artie recalled how the Phantom had launched that bust at Mr Seaton and it seemed only too likely that the invisible fiend was making a similar attack on them. His heart was hammering, but he tried to stay calm.

"Steady, Ham. We need to find a way out."

Step by careful step, they backed away from the unseen menace. Artie could feel Ham trembling at his side.

There came a shattering crash as another box hit the floor and smashed open. The boys swivelled this way and that, trying to spot some sign of their enemy. Both were seized by an overwhelming panic at the prospect of falling victim to the villain's fearsome powers.

"He's coming for us, Artie!" Ham cried. "Run for it!"

He bolted, his shoulder bashing into the shelves and dislodging more boxes as he stumbled along. Artie tried to catch up but lost sight of his friend among the shadows. He ran straight into an immovable wall of packing cases, bashing his nose and reeling back.

Above the pounding of his heart Artie could hear the rasping breath of some unseen menace closing in on him. Before he could turn, he was seized by powerful hands and flung to the floor. As he attempted to rise, he was engulfed in a coarse sack, his arms pinned to his sides.

His struggles proved futile as he was lifted up and carried away as helpless as a fish in a net.

Already stunned by his collision with the packing cases, he was enveloped in the suffocating darkness and passed out. His last thought was that he had proved to be a poor excuse for a detective and he could only hope that Ham had somehow manage to escape the doom he was now being carried towards.

When his senses returned, Artie was still wrapped in the absolute darkness of the sack that had been pulled over his head and all the way down to his waist. He gradually became aware that he was seated in a chair and a firm pair of hands were holding him upright by the shoulders. As he stirred, the hands shifted their grip and yanked the sack from him.

Artie blinked in the light. He had expected to find himself in a dungeon, but what he saw about him was a total surprise. It was a large, bright room with colourful landscape paintings decorating the walls. Delicate porcelain ornaments were perched on shelves at various points, and beneath his feet was a lush Persian carpet.

He was relieved to see Ham seated in a chair to his left. He had also just been freed from a sack, and though it looked like he too had been roughly handled, he had taken no serious harm. With a start, Artie saw that looming behind them was a tall, powerful-looking man in a turban. His dark face was framed in a magnificent beard, and a gold-handled dagger was stuck in the crimson sash wrapped around his waist.

A resonant voice spoke. "May I introduce you to Mr Rajpal Singh, an associate of mine from India." It came from an imposing figure who regarded them steadily from the other side of a large ornate desk. He was seated comfortably in a big leather chair, designed to accommodate his huge bulk. His head was completely bald, while below his broad nose hung a long, white moustache, with a small tuft of beard decorating his round chin. He was dressed in a suit of immaculate white, a yellow shirt with a stiff collar, and a floral silk tie fixed with a jewelled pin. To his left, a caged canary tweeted happily, as though delighting in the boys' discomfort.

Without shifting from his comfortable position, the bald-headed man gazed back and forth between Artie and Ham. In a voice that was surprisingly soft coming from one so large, he said, "Good afternoon, gentlemen. My name is Figg, Cadwallader Figg."

"Figg!" Ham wheezed. "But you're a crim–" He bit back on the word just in time. "I mean you're a notori– Er... I mean you... you..."

"I believe you are trying to say that I am a prominent businessman," Figg filled in placidly, "a dealer in antiques, an importer of finest-quality tea, and occasionally a wine merchant."

"Yes, that's exactly what he meant," Artie agreed.

If this man was truly the criminal mastermind Ferryman had warned them of, it might be more than their lives were worth to make any reference to his illegal activities. In fact, the less they gave away, especially about themselves, the better.

"And you young gentlemen would be?" Figg prompted.

Artie thought for a moment, then answered, "My name is Root, Beresford Root." He glanced over at Ham, hoping he understood the need for false names. "And this is my friend Odys—"

"Bloggs," Ham cut in sharply, "Dickie Bloggs. And I am not a seaman. In fact, I've never even been to sea."

Artie gave an exasperated sigh. Ham clearly disliked the name Odysseus Plank, but at least he had not given his real name.

"We're just harmless schoolboys out for a stroll by the harbour," Artie continued, doing his best to sound like a simple innocent.

"Yes, completely harmless," Ham affirmed. "We're so harmless it's almost ridiculous. We couldn't even hurt ourselves if we tried."

"Schoolboys, you say?" Figg quizzed.

"Yes, we're pupils at Whackford Academy," said Artie, inventing an imaginary school. "School's off for the summer, of course, so we were just out for a wander."

"Yes, rather aimless actually," said Ham. "In fact, I think we got lost. I have no idea where we are and so I couldn't possibly tell anyone about it. If there were anything to tell – which there isn't."

Artie's jaw tightened as he willed Ham to stop gibbering.

Figg regarded them in intimidating silence for almost a full minute before he spoke again in a menacing rumble that made Artie's blood run cold. "Whatever your intentions, I must now decide what is to be done with you."

12.

Pure Humbug

Artie swallowed hard. "Done with us?"

A frown creased Cadwallader Figg's expansive brow. "You were apprehended trespassing on my property. That is intolerable, young man, quite intolerable."

Before Artie could think of a better excuse, Ham blurted out, "We were chasing after my dog, my dog Sebastian. He got loose and ran into the building, so as you can see, we were actually trying to save you trouble by fetching him out."

Figg raised an eyebrow. "A dog, you say? My men made no report of a dog."

"He's a very small dog," said Ham. "They probably didn't notice him because he's so small."

"What breed?" Figg inquired.

"A spaniel," said Artie.

"A poodle," said Ham at the same time.

"Come now, you are making no sense," Figg chided them.

"He's a mixed breed," said Ham. "It's called a spoodle. Or a spandle if you prefer. Or... or..."

Figg raised a hand to silence him and the barest hint of a smile touched his full lips. "You amuse me, sir, you amuse me. You are, if I may say so, a character."

"This has all been a misunderstanding," said Artie, hoping to take advantage of the large man's softening mood. "We really should go now and not take up any more of your time."

He tried to rise, but Rajpal Singh's firm hand pressed him back down in the chair.

"Come, come, Mr Root," said Figg in a darker tone, "such flummery really will not serve you well. This notebook was discovered in your pocket." He laid Artie's notebook open on the desk in front of him and placed a chubby finger on the page. "Allow me to read out one extraordinary extract."

From The Adventures of Beresford Root

As he strode across the dark graveyard to face his arch-enemy, Beresford Root wished he had remembered to bring his pistol. From the other side of the graveyard came the evil Captain Carlton Thrash. The villain stroked his moustache and let out a devilish laugh.

"So, Root, I see you were foolish enough to face me alone," he mocked. "And here am I with three ruthless henchmen, each one a skilled assassin."

"Even if you have an army, it will not avail you, Thrash," countered Beresford. "Right will always triumph over crime."

At that moment, Beresford's stalwart companion Odysseus Plank emerged from the shadows of a tree and stepped to his friend's side. "Well spoken, Beresford." He brandished the heavy wooden cudgel he always carried. "Now let's teach these ruffians the lesson they so richly deserve."

Not for the first time, Beresford was glad to have the portly seaman at his side. With a companion like this, he truly had nothing to fear.

Artie attempted a carefree laugh but was aware of how hollow it sounded. "It's just a story – you know, a bit of fun. Nothing wrong with a chap building himself up a bit, is there?"

Without looking up, Figg turned the page. "There are also a number of references to the crimes of the so-called Scarlet Phantom."

Feeling himself cornered, Artie decided he had to confess some of the truth. "We're investigators, amateur investigators of course. It's sort of a hobby."

"Yes, wherever there's a mystery," Ham chimed in, "you'll find us there, messing about."

"Ghosts, legendary monsters, that sort of thing," said Artie.

"We were going to go fishing for the Loch Ness Monster," said Ham, "but my rod broke."

Artie wished, not for the first time, that he could make Ham keep his mouth shut and leave the talking to him.

Figg raised an eyebrow. "So you decided to investigate this Phantom?"

"Yes," Artie agreed, "just for a lark, of course."

"Why then do you have the addresses of two of my business establishments listed here? Is this unconnected with your investigation or did you hope to discover the unseen robber hiding on my property?" Figg jabbed his finger at the page so forcefully, Artie almost jumped.

As his mind raced to invent an excuse, the door opened to admit an elegant Chinese woman in patterned silk with a rose tucked into her silver hair. Artie had never in his life been so thankful of an interruption. She set a tray with a porcelain tea set and a plate of sesame-seed cakes down in front of Figg.

"Thank you, Mrs Chen," said Figg politely, as she poured him a cup of aromatic tea.

109

When the woman cast a questioning glance in the direction of Artie and Ham, Figg shook his head. "No, Mrs Chen, nothing for my guests at present."

Mrs Chen made a tiny bow and departed, gliding over the carpet as silently as if she was walking on air. Even the door barely made a sound as it closed behind her.

Figg took a sip of tea and began feeding pieces of cake to the canary through the bars of its cage. It tweeted merrily in response.

"As you are a man of some means," said Artie, hoping that his afternoon tea would put the emperor of crime in a merciful mood, "it occurred to us that you... might be the Phantom's next victim."

"Yes, yes," Ham added in support, "and we certainly wouldn't want that to happen."

"Me? A victim?" Figg gave a rich chortle. "I think not. My security, as you have discovered, is absolutely first class."

"Against us," said Artie, "but would it be so effective against an invisible man?"

"Who can walk through walls," Ham added.

"Pshaw!" Figg scoffed. "Invisible man indeed! It is pure humbug! If anyone were capable of such prodigious feats, don't you think I would know about it?"

"Of course you would," said Ham, "because you are the emp–" He stopped himself just in time. "Because you are... a tea merchant."

"Exactly." Figg regarded them pensively. "Do you take the two victims of these crimes for honest men?"

"We've no reason to suppose they're not," said Artie, though he had wondered about this himself.

Figg paused to nibble on a piece of cake. "No, I suppose you have no such reason. But then there is no insurance against dishonesty."

He pulled a yellow kerchief from his breast pocket and dabbed a crumb from his lip. "As a businessman, I am of course interested in the activities of this supposedly invisible cutpurse. It disturbs me that such criminal opportunism should be carried out under my very nose, so to speak. That being the case, should you find some evidence of the identity of the Phantom, I hope you will be so kind as to share that information with me."

Artie froze for a moment, feeling the full force of Figg's intense gaze press upon him. "Well, yes, of course," he managed to say at last, nodding convulsively.

"In that case," Figg concluded, "our business here is done. Mr Singh will escort you to the front door."

The towering Sikh bodyguard grabbed them each by the shoulder and pulled them to their feet. At a signal from Figg, he retrieved the notebook and thrust it into Artie's pocket.

As they were ushered out of the room, Artie heard Figg say, "I shall, of course, be following your activities with great interest."

Once they were out on the street, Artie breathed an immense sigh of relief. They walked briskly away, putting as much distance as possible between themselves and the criminal mastermind's unusual household.

"Artie, you're not really going to report back to Figg, are you?" Ham asked.

"I should say not." Artie repressed a shudder. "I intend to keep as far away from that gentleman as possible."

"You don't think he's the Phantom then?"

"He'd have a lot of trouble making his bulky body invisible. Also, if he's already at the centre of as much crime as the Ferret says he is, as well as running a couple of legitimate businesses, why should he go to the trouble of inventing an invisible man just to get his hands on some jewels?"

"Criminal or not," Ham grumbled, as they followed the road back into town, "you'd think he might have offered us some of that cake."

"We're lucky he didn't have us nailed inside a crate and tossed into the harbour," said Artie with feeling.

"Lucky? Artie, are you forgetting that in the storehouse we were actually attacked by the Scarlet Phantom?"

Artie recalled the shadowy figure that had seized them in the dark, but wondered now what had actually happened. "Are you sure of that?"

"He was tossing boxes at us just the way you said he threw that bust at Mr Seaton," Ham insisted. "What more proof do you need?"

"That wasn't the Scarlet Phantom, you dunce," said a familiar voice, "it was me."

The boys whirled round to see Peril gazing at them with a superior look on her face.

"What are *you* doing here?" Artie demanded. He didn't know whether he was more outraged than surprised that she had sneaked up behind them unnoticed.

"I was making some inquiries of my own about this man Figg," Peril informed them, "when I spotted the two of you creeping about like a pair of incompetent burglars. I decided to watch what you were up to, and, of course, you got yourselves in trouble."

"Are you saying you got through that window all by yourself?" Ham was affronted. He couldn't believe a tiny girl like her could make the climb.

"Don't be so silly," Peril answered, taking a thin piece of wire from her pocket. "I picked the lock with this and came in through the back door."

"You picked the lock?" Artie stared at her. "That's rather an unusual talent."

"For an honest person," Ham added accusingly.

"My mother is constantly mislaying her house keys," Peril explained, "so I taught myself to pick locks to keep from ever being shut out of our own house. Necessity is the mother of invention, as they say."

"Do you always carry a lock-pick with you?" Artie wondered.

"If you two are going to be real detectives," Peril told him primly, "you will need to get yourselves the proper equipment."

"So what about the falling boxes?" Ham reminded her. "Why were you dropping them on us?"

"Oh, yes, well, that was an accident," said Peril, somewhat embarrassed. "It was very dark and I stumbled into those shelves while you were on the other side. I must have jarred some of the boxes so they fell off."

"Well, you scared the life out of us!" Ham fumed.

"And you brought Figg's men down on us," said Artie.

"Yes, I'm sorry about that, but you don't seem any the worse for wear."

"But you told me the Ferret was just making up all that stuff about Cadwallader Figg," said Artie.

"I just wanted the chance to investigate him on my own without you two blundering into it," said Peril haughtily.

"It seems like you were the one doing the blundering," said Ham.

"Alright, alright, but did you find anything out?" Peril asked.

"Well, if Figg is involved with the Phantom, he's doing a good job of covering it up," said Artie. "Look, we'd best go and see if Inspector McCorkle has any new leads."

On the way to the Police Office Artie gave Peril a brief account of their conversation with Cadwallader Figg.

"So did you find anything out?" he asked her.

"I'm afraid not. When I heard those men coming to investigate the falling boxes, I squeezed myself into a corner and stayed hidden until I was sure the coast was clear. I heard them carrying you off, so I waited outside for you to come out."

"And supposing we hadn't come out?" said Ham.

"I would have fetched the police, of course," Peril assured him.

"From now on," said Artie, "we need to stick together. This business is starting to get dangerous."

"You're right," Peril agreed. "From now on we'll pool our resources."

As soon as they walked through the front door of the Police Office they were greeted eagerly by Constable Pennycook. "Ah, Mr Doyle, it is very good to see you. And these friends of yours are...?"

As soon as Artie had introduced Ham and Peril, the young policeman nodded excitedly.

"You've arrived at just the right time," he informed them. "Another warning has been received. The Phantom intends to strike again!"

13.

The Cogitations of Constable Pennycook

"Another warning!" Artie was heartened by the hope this would give him a fresh opportunity to expose the unseen robber.

"Yes, and this time he has gone so far as to threaten one of our leading citizens," said Constable Pennycook. "Sir Archibald Gillybrand."

"The former Lord Provost?" said Peril. "That will make a splash."

"Sir Archibald is talking with the inspector right now," said the young policeman. Beckoning them to follow, he led the way to his superior's office. He rapped on the door and led them inside.

"Doyle, Hamilton and Abernethy, sir," he announced.

Artie saw at a glance that an uncomfortable scene was in progress. Inspector McCorkle was standing and shuffling his feet unhappily. He fidgeted with his watch chain as he faced a barrage of questions from the former Lord Provost, a round gentleman with silver side-whiskers, his thumbs thrust aggressively into the pockets of his brocaded waistcoat.

"Do you mean to tell me that those ridiculous reports in the press are true?" he demanded. "Do you expect me to believe that there is an invisible fiend on the loose in Edinburgh? Can it possibly be the case that the police are not up to the task of capturing this thief?"

"Ah, Mr Doyle," the inspector greeted the newcomers. He was clearly glad of the interruption. "This warning was slipped under the front door of Sir Archibald's house this morning."

He picked up a card from his desk and handed it to Artie. In the familiar red ink were written the words,

You will be my
third victim
tomorrow night
at ten o'clock

"Who on earth are these young people?" Sir Archibald was red in the face. "Do you have school groups traipsing through your office, Inspector? No wonder crime runs rampant!"

"Such is the importance of this case," said McCorkle apologetically, "we are employing every possible resource, however unorthodox."

"Are you and your men so incompetent that you are handing the matter over to children?" Sir Archibald fumed. "Can you find no clues? Will you resort to reading tea leaves next?"

When the former Lord Provost paused for breath, the inspector said, "It is a very unusual case, Your Honour. The witnesses are all agreed."

"Agreed?" Sir Archibald was scornful. "Agreed on what?"

"Agreed," the inspector responded feebly, "that they did not see the thief."

"Well that's a fine thing!" Sir Archibald huffed disgustedly. "You and your men are simply baffled?"

"Perhaps not, sir," Constable Pennycook interjected. "I have attempted once more to duplicate the thought processes of Mr Poe's fictional detective C. Auguste Dupin."

McCorkle eyed his subordinate with smouldering disfavour. "If you once more attempt to tell me what thoughts are running through my own head," he warned,

"I shall lock you in a cell myself and throw away the key."

"No, no, sir," said Pennycook, "I am applying Monsieur Dupin's methods to the facts of the case. I have been cogitating, so to speak, and I have reached a definite conclusion."

Artie was intrigued. He wondered if the young policeman really had solved the case. "And what conclusion is that?" he asked.

Pennycook allowed himself a dramatic pause. "The Scarlet Phantom is not a human being at all. He is, in fact – a monkey."

McCorkle's eyebrows shot up in stupefied amazement. "You can't possibly be serious!"

"Look at the evidence, sir. If you review the facts as Monsieur Dupin would, why, the truth simply leaps out at you."

Ham leaned forward. "A monkey?" His smile told Artie that his friend rather liked the idea.

Sir Archibald stared incredulously at the constable, as though he were some strange creature just arrived from the moon.

"I can't say I follow your reasoning," said Peril, "and I doubt if anyone else can either."

Pennycook wagged a finger in the air as though he were giving a lecture. "Let us begin with the first robbery. In a crowded street, a monkey, scampering along at knee level, might well pass unnoticed by people whose eyes were fixed on shop windows or the faces of their companions."

The inspector made a strangled noise in his throat, but Pennycook continued with mounting enthusiasm.

"Now, granted that he has the strength of a jungle beast, our monkey could easily knock a man down so quickly that the victim would be unable to identify his assailant. With his nimble fingers he could snatch the necklace from the jeweller's pocket and, with his natural agility, disappear over the nearest wall."

A dead silence ensued. Pennycook looked in vain to his audience for some sign of approval.

Artie drew a deep breath. "But the second robbery wasn't out in the open," he pointed out. "It was in a locked room with no way in or out."

"That is not exactly correct," said Pennycook. "Remember there was a fireplace, and while we established that the chimney was too narrow for a man to slide down, it would be a simple matter for a monkey to enter the room by that route."

"And he threw the bust of Wellington at Mr Seaton," said Ham, enthusiastically supporting the constable, "stunning him before he realised that there was someone – or something – in the room."

"Exactly!" Pennycook's chest swelled with pride at his own ingenuity.

"I'm still not clear how a monkey could open a safe," said Peril dubiously.

"There is only one possible solution to that," said Pennycook, quite unruffled. "Mr Seaton did not lock the safe properly in the first place, so it was an easy matter for the monkey to reach inside, snatch the jewels and scramble back up the chimney. When questioned, Seaton was too embarrassed to admit his carelessness."

Inspector McCorkle was chewing agitatedly on his moustache. It was clear he was itching to denounce the constable's outlandish theory but unable to offer a better one.

"I have to say this sounds like an awfully intelligent monkey," said Artie.

"Not at all," Pennycook informed him. "It has merely been trained to perform these actions by the brilliant villain who masterminded the crime."

"I don't suppose you can tell us who that is?" McCorkle growled.

Pennycook's face fell. "My cogitations have not yet extended that far. But I do have a plan to frustrate his next nefarious exploit."

"What is your plan?" Ham asked excitedly.

"It is this," Pennycook explained. "We scatter bananas all around the intended scene of the crime. The monkey, being a simple animal, will be unable to resist the fruit, and when he stops to feed, we throw a net over him and so bring the Phantom's reign of terror to an end."

At this, Sir Archibald exploded in fury. "What nonsense is this? Bananas! Monkeys! Are you trying to turn my home into some sort of a circus?"

"Only for your own protection, sir," the abashed Pennycook responded.

"Be quiet, Pennycook!" the inspector ordered brusquely. "We'll have no more of these havers."

While the policemen tried to placate the outraged Sir Archibald, Ham drew Artie aside. "Artie, that chap Figg imports all sorts of things from abroad. He could easily have brought in a trained monkey from Africa or Borneo."

Artie shook his head. "I know we want an answer to this mystery, but I really can't swallow the idea that it's a monkey doing all this."

"It makes no sense at all," Peril agreed. "Look at it logically. If this monkey is so small that nobody noticed it scampering around in the street, then it would hardly be big enough to overpower two grown men."

"I suppose not," Ham admitted.

"And if this is just about stealing some jewels," said Artie, "why go to the bother of sending warnings in advance?"

At that moment the door opened and a short, stout man entered the room and looked about him with an air of officious authority. With an inward groan, Artie recognised him as the inspector's superior, Lieutenant Sneddon, a man who always thought he knew more than anyone else but never actually did.

McCorkle snapped to attention. "Good day, sir. I was just assuring Sir Archibald that we will be offering him the best possible protection."

Sneddon treated the three youngsters to a disdainful glance. "I've allowed you a certain amount of latitude, McCorkle, given the extraordinary circumstances of the case. However, your bumbling approach has yielded no results whatsoever."

Pennycook was about to open his mouth but the inspector silenced him with an angry gesture.

"We do have one or two leads," Artie protested.

"Your services are no longer required, Mr Doyle," Sneddon retorted curtly. "We now have the assistance of an expert in these esoteric matters."

As he spoke a small, wiry man with a hooked nose and a wild shock of grey hair entered the room.

"May I present Mr Daffyd Pendragon – the noted paranormal investigator."

14.

The Powers of Pendragon

The newcomer gave a small bow as he entered Inspector McCorkle's office and spoke in a lilting Welsh accent. "In this crisis I am entirely at your disposal, gentlemen. As is my invaluable and gifted assistant, my daughter Rose-Ivy."

He was followed into the room by a thin, flaxen-haired girl of about fifteen, whose wide blue eyes drifted about the room without fixing on any particular object. She smiled wanly at her father's compliment.

The former Lord Provost scowled. "Lieutenant Sneddon, are you asking me to believe that we face some sort of malevolent spirit?"

"That has yet to be determined," said the lieutenant, "since the inspector here is no closer to apprehending the culprit than he was on the first day. Don't fret, Your Honour. Your house will be surrounded by a cordon of policemen, but it does not hurt to cover all eventualities."

"And this gentleman?" Sir Archibald twitched a finger in the direction of Daffyd Pendragon.

"He comes with the most persuasive credentials," said Sneddon. "Letters of commendation from the likes of Lord Cairncross and the Duke of Strathdonnan."

"I have been of some service to those gentlemen," Pendragon affirmed modestly, "and to many others."

"I did hear that you lifted a curse from the duke's ancestral castle," said Sir Archibald, slightly mollified.

"And dispersed the ghostly manifestations which were causing such mischief on the estate of Lord Cairncross," the Welshman added. "I also have testimonials from numerous prestigious persons across the length and breadth of our kingdom, from Orkney to Cornwall."

Peril could not contain a contemptuous snort. "It's all pure nonsense, a mixture of fevered imaginations and cheap parlour tricks."

"Ah, we have a sceptic in our midst," Pendragon retorted mildly. "Young lady, ghosts, poltergeists, wandering spirits – the evidence for their existence is overwhelming. You find tales of their presence in the writings of Plutarch, Pliny and other classical authors. Every culture, from the most primitive to the most civilised, has testified to the haunting power of spirit beings, and called them by a hundred different names – ghosts, goblins, demons, fairies… And then there are those who draw power from them: sorcerers they were called once, but my term for them is 'psychic practitioners'."

"Utter tosh!" Peril declared. "There's not a shred of practical evidence for any of it."

Rose-Ivy's large eyes fixed upon the other girl as though staring at her through a telescope. "She has a troubled spirit," she lilted in an ethereal voice. "An aura of tragedy hangs about her."

Peril was momentarily taken aback, but then she glowered fiercely. "You keep your auras to yourself. If this mystery is to be solved and the thief cornered, it needs to be done on the basis of reason and science, not clouded with superstition."

"Clearly you do not realise that the investigation of psychic phenomena has in recent years become a science in its own right," Pendragon explained with exaggerated patience, "with methods as regulated and well defined as those of physics or chemistry."

"Peril, we should at least give him a chance," Artie muttered.

"Yes, if we're to face a ghost," Ham agreed, "I'd like to have an expert on hand."

"I wouldn't mind a chance to test these *methods* of his for myself," said Peril. "I'd show it all up for the balderdash it is."

"Do you have a working theory, Mr Pendragon, as to how the Scarlet Phantom commits these extraordinary crimes?" Inspector McCorkle inquired.

"In the far-off East, in the temples of India and Tibet," said the Welshman, "there are mystics who, by the practice of meditation, have performed astonishing feats. With my own eyes I have seen them walk barefoot over hot coals and even float in the air several inches above the ground."

Artie could tell that Peril was aching to heap scorn on the Welshman, but she merely crossed her arms and seethed in silence.

Pendragon hunched his shoulders as though against a cold wind, and his tone grew sombre. "We may be facing an ectoplasmic projection, see."

"Perhaps you might explain that," Sneddon requested, "for the benefit of those of us not closely acquainted with paranormal phenomena."

"Well then, like blood, breath and water, ectoplasm is one of the substances that make up the human body," said Pendragon. "In fact, it's what holds all the others together. It is of a nature midway between the physical and the spiritual and is able to adopt the attributes of either, becoming immaterial in order to pass through walls, then material in order to move or grasp solid objects."

Artie found himself becoming quite fascinated by the

Welshman's theories. "And do you have any such abilities yourself, Mr Pendragon?" he inquired.

"No, but my daughter Rose-Ivy has a certain psychic talent. She is able to detect the presence of discarnate entities."

"Disparate whats?" asked Ham.

"Spirits," Pendragon explained. "She is sensitive to their psychic vibrations and assists me in tracking them down."

Rose-Ivy had been hovering behind her father like some ghostly moth. Now she stepped forward with a faraway look in her eyes and spoke in a high, lilting voice. "I sense unhappy spirits, cast out of the fairy realm to wander the earth, gathering treasure for their queen, that is Queen Mab, who dwells in a palace spun from gossamer and dewdrops. She flies in a chariot drawn by fireflies, passing through the dreams of men to rob them of their fancies. At her passing, horses and cattle fall into a swoon and babies wake crying from their sleep."

"I think that's enough, Rosie," Pendragon interrupted gently. "We don't want to keep everyone awake with nightmares."

"I'm not entirely convinced by all this," Sir Archibald announced stiffly, "but tell me what steps you intend to take to thwart this villain."

"Ah well, all these disembodied forces operate through vibrations in the ether," the Welshman explained. "*Ether* being the term we use to describe the field of energy which fills all of space. I have constructed a device which can detect, block and even disperse those etheric frequencies. By such means I can offer you complete psychic protection."

"And with a strong police presence," Sneddon chipped in, "we can fully guarantee to frustrate whatever this crook has in mind."

"Well, Mr Pendragon's plan certainly sounds more sensible than filling my house with bananas." Sir Archibald threw Constable Pennycook a withering look.

"If the Phantom intends to strike at ten o'clock tomorrow night," said McCorkle, attempting to recover some semblance of authority, "we should arrive at least two hours in advance in order to secure the premises and allow Mr Pendragon to set up his equipment."

"We'll be there too," Artie put in hastily, "to look out for any clues to the Phantom's identity."

"You will not," Sneddon retorted flatly. "I'll not have children playing around in the midst of a serious police operation."

Artie's heart sank and he saw glum looks on the faces of his two friends. Then, unexpectedly, Pendragon spoke up.

"On the contrary, let them come along. I think the more witnesses there are to whatever takes place, the better. It might be a lesson for any unbelievers."

"Thank you, Mr Pendragon," said Artie. He was grateful that Peril was keeping her mouth shut so as not to ruin this opportunity.

"You'll hardly even know we're there," Ham assured the psychic investigator. "By the way, will there be sandwiches?"

When they left the Police Office and made their way along the High Street, Peril was still fuming.

"Ectoplasm indeed!" she sneered. "I never heard such gibberish."

"You know what Shakespeare said, Peril," Artie told her. "'There are more things in heaven and earth than are dreamt of in your philosophy.'"

"It will be a fine day when I have to take advice from a playwright," Peril declared stubbornly.

"I don't know, Peril," said Ham. "Pendragon sounded awfully convincing to me."

"That's because you'll swallow any nonsense if it sounds exciting enough," Peril sniffed. "It's all just a way of extorting money from the gullible. You persuade them that a few random accidents in their home are the result of a curse or some invading ghost, then you convince them that you can put an end to their troubles with some psychic mumbo-jumbo. So long as they can pay the fee, of course."

"And Mr Daffyd Pendragon has been very well paid by some of his wealthy clients," put in a voice.

Johnny Ferryman stepped out of a doorway right into their path. "So, Mr Doyle, have you any new information to offer me?"

"If you're referring to that large gentleman whose name you gave us," said Artie – he avoided saying Figg's name out loud in a public place – "I don't think there's anything to be gained from following him around."

"I was thinking more of Pendragon," said the reporter. "I suppose he's been brought in to protect our former Lord Provost."

"How did you know about that?" asked Artie.

"Sir Archibald's not one to keep mum about somebody threatening him," the Ferret explained. "His servants have been blabbing about it all over town. When I saw our former Lord Provost go into the Police Office and then Pendragon, it was obvious what's going on. So what can you tell me about your little meeting in there, Mr Doyle?" He plucked a pencil from behind his ear and pointed it in the direction of the Police Office.

"Lieutenant Sneddon wanted us off the case," said Artie, "but Pendragon said we should be present as witnesses at Sir Archibald's house tomorrow night."

"I hope you can provide me with a few details of whatever occurs," said the Ferret. "Perhaps a first-hand account of the psychic battle between the Scarlet Phantom and Daffyd Pendragon."

Artie was reluctant to become further involved with the prying reporter. "Maybe you should speak to Mr Pendragon himself," he suggested.

"Chance would be a fine thing," said Ferryman. "As soon as I heard he was back in town, I went straight to his house in Broughton Road. Can't miss it. There's an ugly stone gargoyle mounted over the front door. When I tried to get an interview I was chased off by the most ferocious housekeeper I ever set eyes on – a real harpy."

"It seems to me," said Peril, "that if there is somebody behind these robberies, it's Pendragon himself. After all, he makes his living from fakery and so he might know exactly how to pull off these seemingly impossible crimes."

"Actually, Peril, that makes a lot of sense," said Artie. "He could just be pretending to help the police so that nobody will suspect him."

Ferryman shook his head. "Sorry, girly. You're barking up the wrong tree there. I already sent a telegram to one of my colleagues on the *Aberdeen Herald* to check. He confirmed that for the past week Pendragon's been giving lectures up there – daughter in attendance too. There is no way they could have travelled down here to commit the robberies, not without their absence being noted."

"So much for that theory," said Ham. "I still say it's a ghost." He pondered for a moment. "Possibly conjured up by a witch."

"Well, I say nothing at all will happen tomorrow night," Peril asserted firmly. "It's all stuff and nonsense."

"I don't know about that," said Artie. "I've got a hunch that this mystery is about to get even deeper."

The Fateful Hour

Who is the Scarlet Phantom?

- *Royston Kincaid – why steal own jewels?*
- *Miss Toner – not very nice*
- *Reginald Seaton – injured by attacker*
- *Hubert Simpkin – unlikely but…*
- *Ferret – wants a story*
- *Mrs Abernethy – surely not!*
- *Inspector McCorkle – impossible*
- *Pendragon – absent in Aberdeen during robberies*
- *Rose-Ivy – creepy, but as above*
- *C.F. (crim. mas.) – very dangerous*
- *Lieutenant Sneddon – not around when Phantom attacks*

Artie had a last look at his notes before entering Sir
Archibald's house and slipping the notebook back in his
pocket. He had never seen so many policemen. There
were three of them posted at the gate leading to the
grounds of the large house in Belgrave Crescent. Every
door into the building was guarded by two constables,
with one stationed outside every single room.

"There must be no police at all anywhere else in the
city," said Ham. "It's like they're expecting an invasion."

"Yes, but not from a foreign country," said Artie, "from
the spirit world."

"I haven't seen that Lieutenant Sneddon anywhere
around, though," Peril noted.

"I hear he claimed to have an important appointment
in Prestonpans," said Artie. "That way if the Phantom
should be captured, he can claim the credit of having
made the arrangements, but if the result is another fiasco,
he can lay all the blame on Inspector McCorkle."

When they entered the front parlour, Peril tried to
examine the machine Pendragon was setting up, but the
Welshman shooed her away angrily. "I won't have you

disturbing this delicate mechanism!" he warned.

The three youngsters were squeezed onto a divan with orders not to move from that spot. Sir Archibald was pacing impatiently back and forth while puffing on a thin black cigar. Inspector McCorkle and Constable Pennycook observed him warily, as if at any moment he might explode into an ill-tempered fireball.

On a table in the centre of the room sat a locked strongbox in which the former Lord Provost had placed all the jewellery in the house: a pearl necklace, several brooches studded with emeralds and sapphires, and various other valuable items. To one side of the table, Daffyd Pendragon was bent over a machine he referred to as an 'etheric galvanator' while he made a few final adjustments to the mechanism.

It was a metal box the size of a dressing table, with a glassy screen on top in place of a mirror. A number of lenses protruded from it, and there were rows of knobs which Pendragon was setting with utmost care. As he did so, he eyed the several dials on the top of the machine, the needles of which quivered as he worked. At his side his daughter stood, swaying slowly from side to side, as though in time to music only she could hear.

The former Lord Provost suddenly rounded on the Welshman. "Are you not yet done tinkering with that infernal contraption?"

Pendragon cast a glance at the clock on the mantlepiece, which displayed the time as ten minutes before ten – very close now to the hour the Scarlet Phantom threatened to strike.

"The instrument is very sensitive," he said, "and I must make delicate adjustments to ensure maximum effectiveness. I need to take into account the temperature of the room, the magnetic fields surrounding the house, and the fluctuating energy auras of everyone present."

Satisfied at last, he straightened and pressed down on a brass lever. A deep electrical hum started up from somewhere in the depths of the metallic casing, and the glass screen began to glow with a pale green light.

"Could you explain to us again exactly what you are aiming to achieve?" Inspector McCorkle requested.

"Having carefully examined all the statements relating to the Scarlet Phantom's first two attacks," Pendragon answered, "I now have a clearer impression of the particular esoteric powers he brings to bear."

"More claptrap," Peril muttered under her breath.

Artie shushed her, afraid that if she upset the psychic investigator they might be thrown out of the room before the fateful hour arrived.

"I would theorise that he has mastered the ability to control the very atoms of his body," the Welshman continued. "In this way he is able, with great concentration, to divert light rays around him, thus rendering himself invisible. With an even more intense effort he is able to dematerialise for short periods, long enough to pass through solid objects."

"And what will this machine of yours do?" wondered Constable Pennycook, gazing at the mechanism with boyish curiosity.

"Here it comes," Peril murmured, "more gibberish."

"It generates an etheric field which will detect and pinpoint the location of the Phantom," the Welshman replied. "This field of highly charged energy will keep him at bay, and, when power is increased, entrap him like a fish in a net."

"There's no chance he'll just go ghostly and slip away?" McCorkle sounded anxious, fearing another failure.

"If my calculations are correct," Pendragon assured him, "then the galvanic charge will force him to become corporeal – that is, solid – even in his invisible state, making it possible to restrain and capture him."

"It sounds to me like that will make him more dangerous," Ham murmured.

"Let's just hope Pendragon knows what he's doing," said Artie.

Peril made a grumpy noise and thrust her hands into her pockets.

"Now everyone keep still and be quiet," the Welshman ordered. "We can't risk any disturbance in the galvanic emanations."

Sir Archibald slumped into an armchair and chewed on his cigar, while Inspector McCorkle and Constable Pennycook stood stiffly to attention by the fireplace, like a pair of sentries on guard. The only sounds Artie could hear now were the beating of his own heart, the low hum of the machine, and the slow ticking of the clock as the last few minutes slipped by.

Silence pressed down on the room like the heavy atmosphere of an approaching thunderstorm. As the hands on the clock drew closer to ten, Artie was aware of Ham's breath beside him growing more nervous, while on his other side Peril was tensed for an attack by a ghostly figure she claimed not to believe in. His greatest anxiety was that after all this preparation, with the trap in place, the Phantom might not appear at all, and it would all be in vain.

At the first chime of the hour, Artie's head instinctively jerked round to face the door, as if it might suddenly burst open to admit the invisible fiend.

TWO, THREE, FOUR came the chimes. Artie felt his arms and legs aching with the effort of keeping still, the chimes ringing in his ears like the tolling of a great bell.

FIVE, SIX, SEVEN.

He looked to where Pendragon bent over his machine, gazing intently at the dials, while his daughter stood beside him as rigid as a statue, her huge, unsettling eyes fixed on empty space.

Eight, nine, ten.

When the final chime died away, it was as if every heart in the room had stopped along with it. Artie clenched and unclenched his fists, hardly daring to breathe. On either side of him, Ham and Peril sat fixedly, as if paralysed. The atmosphere in the room crackled with tension.

Suddenly the air was split by a terrible shriek.

"Angels and ministers of grace defend us!"

It was Rose-Ivy, her voice as shrill as the cry of a frightened bird. "He comes! He comes!"

Everyone who was seated shot to their feet and the remains of Sir Archibald's cigar dropped from his gaping mouth. Constable Pennycook drew his truncheon and brandished it defensively in front of him.

"Careful, Constable, careful!" The inspector grabbed the young policeman's arm and pushed it down, but he too looked rattled.

Ham's round face was white as chalk. "Oh, Artie, he's here," he gasped. "The Scarlet Phantom!"

Artie too felt a tingle of horror run down his spine. "Steady, Ham, steady!" he urged.

"There's nothing here," Peril insisted breathlessly. "There can't be." But she sounded as shocked as everyone else.

Pendragon was furiously twisting the knobs on his machine and lights flashed over its metallic surface. "Can you see him, Rosie? Where is he?"

In answer to her father, Rose-Ivy elevated a slender arm and pointed a thin, outstretched finger at a far corner of the room. Her hand moved slowly left and right, as though tracking an unseen target.

"Here he comes – a goblin spirit of wicked intent!" the girl cried. Her high-pitched voice scraped the nerves of everyone in the room. Artie's heart skipped a beat as he swallowed a surge of panic.

"He comes in questionable shape," Rose-Ivy crooned, "making night hideous to shake us beyond the reach of our souls."

"He's more powerful than I imagined!" A cold sweat had broken out on Pendragon's brow. "Quick, everyone, gather round me! The galvanic field is our only protection."

Everyone scurried together in a tight semi-circle around the Welshman. Rose-Ivy's upraised arm dropped to her side and she began to swoon. The inspector and Constable Pennycook caught her just in time to keep her from sinking to the floor.

Artie felt the blood pounding in his temples and fear

rose in his throat with a bitter taste. Ham clutched his arm on one side while Peril clung to the other.

"I have him!" Pendragon announced in a cracked voice. "I have him!"

Everyone stared at the screen on top of the mechanism. In the misty glass a figure could be seen, a wavering human shape that was drawing menacingly closer.

"He is pushing through," Pendragon breathed. "He isn't stopping."

Sir Archibald seized the Welshman by the shoulder. "For heaven's sake, man, protect us!"

The noise of the machine rose to an ear-splitting whine.

"The etheric field is forcing him to manifest," Pendragon announced. "He is vulnerable, but only for a few moments."

Leaving Rose-Ivy slumped against the inspector, Constable Pennycook raised his truncheon. "That's all we need!"

With an angry grunt he hurled the weapon with all his might. Everyone watched dumbfounded as it flew through the empty air to smash a vase on the mantlepiece.

"You missed, Constable!" Pendragon exclaimed. "But I won't!"

From inside his jacket he drew out a pistol. In a flash he extended his arm and pulled the trigger. The boom of his gun shook the room like a thunderbolt.

16.

Hard Evidence

As Pendragon lowered his pistol, the whine of the etheric galvanator subsided to a low hum. Craning forward, Artie saw that the glassy screen was now blank. Rose-Ivy rubbed her brow, as though to clear away the memory of a bad dream.

"He is gone," she keened in a sing-song voice, "back into the mists."

"It looks like you missed too, sir," said Pennycook.

"I'm sure I hit him," said the Welshman, his breath still coming fast. "A flesh wound at least."

Sir Archibald drew out a fresh cigar and lit it with trembling fingers. "That was a hairy business – weirdest thing I ever saw."

"Well, we certainly got the best of him this time," said the inspector, assuming an air of dignified satisfaction, "thanks to you, Mr Pendragon."

"Perhaps, Your Honour," suggested Constable

Pennycook, "you should check the contents of your strongbox, just to be sure."

"You're right, young fellow, quite right," said the former Lord Provost.

He took a key from the pocket of his waistcoat, unlocked the stongbox and raised the lid. For a second Artie had a dreadful fear that somehow the Phantom had managed to snatch the jewels away from right under their noses, and he was relieved when he saw a smile break out on Sir Archibald's face.

"All present and correct, gentlemen. I think we can pronounce this night a success for the forces of law."

Artie edged over to where the broken vase lay in pieces on the floor beside the constable's truncheon. As he approached, his eye was drawn to a small hole in the wall surrounded by cracked plaster. Taking a penknife from his pocket, he pressed the blade into the hole and carefully prised out the bullet. He stared at it lying in the palm of his hand, scarcely able to believe his eyes.

"What's the matter, Artie?" asked Ham. "You look as though you've seen a ghost. I mean… Well, you know what I mean."

He and Peril pressed around their friend to stare at his find.

"Look," said Artie, "this is Mr Pendragon's bullet. It's stained red."

144

Ham's jaw dropped in speechless amazement.

Peril took out her magnifying glass and examined the bullet.

"Is that what I think it is?" Artie asked.

Peril frowned and nodded. "Yes. It's blood."

Pendragon plucked the bullet from Artie's hand and held it out triumphantly for everyone to see. "I knew I hit the fiend! Thanks to my etheric field he was solid enough to be harmed."

"Well, sir," said McCorkle admiringly, "that is hard evidence, hard evidence indeed. There can be no further doubt that we have faced a fiend possessed of preternatural abilities."

"Now that he knows we can spot him and do him harm," said Sir Archibald, blowing a cloud of smoke into the air, "I expect we've seen the last of this villain."

"Do not say so," Rose-Ivy warned in her high, floating voice. "He is, I sense, a determined spirit."

"Well, Peril," said Ham, "it looks like my idea of a ghost was close enough to the truth."

Peril chewed her lower lip and twirled the magnifying glass agitatedly between her fingers. "I don't understand it," she muttered, "I don't understand it at all."

In spite of her hard-headed devotion to science, Artie could see that she was just as shaken by the night's events as everyone else.

"At least now we know we're dealing with a mortal, however gifted," he said, "and he can be stopped. The bloodstained bullet proves that."

As he retrieved his truncheon from the floor, Constable Pennycook leaned close to Artie and spoke to him in a confidential tone. "Mr Doyle, if you and your friends would meet me at noon tomorrow at Mrs McTarry's luncheon room in Victoria Street, I believe I may be able to shed some light on this mysterious business."

Noticing that Ham had overheard, he added, "And yes, Mr Hamilton, lunch will be provided."

Artie nodded a willing agreement. He was quite sure that they were not done with the Scarlet Phantom.

The next day at noon Artie, Ham and Peril kept their appointment. Mrs McTarry's was at the midway point of Victoria Street as it twisted downward towards the Grassmarket. Inside was a plain room with a dozen or so customers eating soup, stew or pie at the round wooden tables. Some were seated on stools at the counter with plates of bread and cheese in front of them. The simple menu was written in chalk on a large blackboard, and Ham ran his eyes over it hungrily as they sat down at an empty table to await Constable Pennycook.

"I don't know about you two," said Ham, "but I could barely sleep last night. Every time I closed my eyes I saw that horrid apparition coming at me with his arms outstretched. My mother eventually made me some hot milk to help me doze off."

"It was pretty unsettling," Artie admitted. "I had one or two bad dreams myself. I certainly didn't tell my parents what happened. My mother would have rounded up an army of bishops with buckets full of holy water."

"You're being very quiet, Peril," said Ham. "That's not like you."

"I talked it over with my mother," said Peril sullenly, "to try to make sense of it. But we couldn't. It's… it's very upsetting."

"Maybe this isn't the sort of mystery a detective can solve," Artie sighed.

With a stubborn frown, Peril planted her elbows on the tabletop. "We have to keep an eye on the facts. Notice that last night the Phantom didn't knock anybody down or throw anything across the room, as he did on previous occasions."

"Only because Pendragon stopped him," said Ham.

"We all saw the image," Artie reminded her, "and the blood on the bullet. Will you still not accept that, however he does it, there is an invisible fiend out there?"

"I can't," Peril declared flatly. "I just can't."

At that moment Constable Pennycook entered and gave them a cheery greeting on his way to the counter. He returned shortly with four mugs of steaming-hot tea and four slices of cold mutton pie.

"Well, Constable," said Artie, stirring milk into his tea, "last night you indicated that you had some thoughts to share. Does that mean you have a new theory?"

"Indeed I do," said Pennycook, "but since my monkey theory did not go down well with the inspector, I thought I would try this new notion out on you three young people first. You are well acquainted with the facts of the case and so are in a good position to judge the soundness of my solution."

"We're very keen to hear it." Artie was genuinely intrigued.

Pennycook bit into his slice of pie and chewed methodically as he gathered his thoughts. Washing it down with a gulp of tea, he looked round at his audience.

"First, I am sure we can all agree that these events, some of which we have witnessed at first hand, appear to be quite impossible."

"I certainly agree with that," said Peril.

"Now, if we take that as our basis," Pennycook continued, "and reason in the manner of Mr Poe's brilliant detective C. Auguste Dupin, we come to the conclusion that they must not have happened at all."

Ham gave a puzzled grunt and Artie was just as baffled.

"I'm not sure I follow your reasoning." Peril adjusted her spectacles, as if that might help her see the young policeman's point.

"I am not yet done deducing." Pennycook took another swallow of tea before resuming. "If these events did not, in fact, occur, then our minds must have been influenced into believing that they did."

"This is giving me a headache," Ham groaned as he munched on his last piece of pie.

"Are you saying it was all an illusion?" Artie asked.

"Produced by magic, I suppose," said Peril scornfully.

"Not at all, young lady," Pennycook corrected her. "It is entirely a matter of science, just as you would have it – the science of mesmerism. Or, to use a more modern term, hypnosis."

"Hypnosis?" said Artie. "Isn't that some sort of sleep?"

"Not exactly," said the constable. "The term was coined by the Scottish doctor James Braid to describe his technique of placing patients in a trance-like state in order to relieve their symptoms through the power of the mind."

"Yes, I've heard of such things," said Peril, "but I don't see what that has to do with these robberies."

"Let me explain," said Pennycook, warming to his subject. "I recently attended a demonstration by the noted medical expert Professor Stone at the Freemasons' Hall.

The professor is an expert in these techniques and demonstrated them on members of the audience onstage. He compelled one person to make a speech in the belief that he was our Prime Minister Mr Gladstone addressing Parliament. Another subject was compelled to dance a jig against his will, while others caused much amusement by ducking to dodge an imaginary flock of owls."

"So you think the Scarlet Phantom is using hypnosis," said Artie.

"Exactly so, Mr Doyle." The young policeman treated himself to a triumphant swallow of tea. "He is expert in an advanced form of the technique which allows him to affect the minds of several people at once."

"I hardly think anyone could use that trick to affect a whole street full of people," Peril objected. "It just isn't possible."

"And Mr Seaton was alone in a locked room," said Artie.

"And there was blood on that bullet," added Ham, tapping a finger on his now empty plate.

"I'm not saying my theory is complete." Pennycook was clearly discomfited. "But I believe it is an avenue worth exploring."

He stood up and popped a last fragment of pie into his mouth. "I must be getting back to the office," he said, putting on his helmet. "Now, if you young people would think on this theory, you might have some notions of who might be our mysterious hypnotist."

Once the policeman had left, Artie looked at his two friends. "Well, it's not as silly an idea as that one about the trained monkey."

"It still doesn't hold water." Peril shook her head. "We know for a fact we weren't hypnotised. If anyone really had that power over people's minds, wouldn't they do a lot more with it than simply steal jewellery?"

"The constable really should give up trying to imitate this Angus Dustbin person," said Ham.

"Auguste Dupin," Artie corrected him. He flipped open his notebook and added this new theory to his list.

Invisible Attack – How?

- ~~Wind~~
- ~~Brain seizure~~
- Invisibility potion
- Mirror suit
- Mechanical device
- Psychic power
- Ghost
- Monkey
- Hypnosis

"Yes, yes, whatever he's called." Ham eyed his friend's plate. "By the way, Artie, if you're not going to finish your pie, can I have it?"

When the meal was over, they left Mrs McTarry's and started up the twisting road. Although Artie was not convinced by Pennycook's hypnosis theory, there was something to what he said. The notion that these events simply could not have happened echoed at the back of Artie's mind like the chiming of a distant bell.

They had just turned into the High Street when they were brought up short by the sight of the young constable dashing excitedly towards them.

"Oh good, I've caught you!" he gasped. "There was a message waiting at the office. The inspector wants us to join him at once."

"Join him where?" asked Artie.

"At the place where the Phantom intends to strike next." Pennycook pointed a finger up the long, straight road. "Edinburgh Castle!"

Even as he spoke, the One o'Clock Gun boomed out from the castle high above, as though sounding a dreadful warning of trouble to come.

17.

The Great Treasure

With Constable Pennycook in the lead, the three youngsters made their way up to the great castle, which sat upon its rugged crag, overlooking the city like a watchful guardian. Over the centuries it had been a mighty fortress in time of war, a prison for captured enemies, and home to some of Scotland's proudest army regiments.

"The Phantom must be mad to try to break into this place," said Artie, gazing at the high walls and stout turrets.

"You're right," Peril agreed. "There are hundreds of soldiers stationed here."

"What on earth does the Phantom want to steal from the castle anyway?" Ham wondered as they walked up the Esplanade towards the gate. "Cannons? Suits of armour?"

"Mr Hamilton," said the constable, "must I remind you that Edinburgh Castle is home to the greatest treasures in the entire country – the Honours of Scotland!"

Once inside, the policeman took them to the palace

building, where kings and queens had resided in past centuries and which now housed the Crown Room. This was a windowless vaulted chamber, its walls panelled with oak and its chimneys secured with iron bars.

Here they found Inspector McCorkle awaiting them with the Pendragons, and an elderly man dressed in a red uniform bedecked with medals. He had the stiff bearing of a veteran officer, and as the newcomers entered, he examined them with a sharp eye, as though they were soldiers on parade.

"May I introduce General Henry Dundas, the governor of Edinburgh Castle," said the inspector.

"Are the ranks of the Edinburgh police so depleted that they must depend on these youthful irregulars?" the general inquired gruffly.

McCorkle ignored the criticism and displayed another of the Scarlet Phantom's cards. "I have just brought the general this message, which was stuck to the door of the Police Office by persons unknown. It reads thusly:

My next target is the great treasure of Scotland. I shall strike at Edinburgh Castle on Saturday night.

The inspector looked up from the card and added grimly, "That is tomorrow night."

"There can be no doubt as to what he means by the great treasure," said General Dundas.

All eyes turned to the glass case which contained the Sword of State, the crown and the sceptre. These were the Scottish crown jewels, usually referred to as the Honours of Scotland.

"In olden times," said Dundas, "these were used in the coronation of every Scottish monarch from Mary, Queen of Scots to Charles the Second."

"Is it true, sir," asked Pennycook, "that they are the oldest crown jewels in the whole of the British Isles?"

"Indeed they are," the general replied proudly. "When Oliver Cromwell declared England a republic in the seventeenth century, he melted down the English crown jewels and turned them into coins. When he came north into Scotland, to prevent him from destroying the Honours they were hidden, first in Dunnottar Castle and then under the floor of Kinneff parish church. After many adventures, they finally came to rest here."

Artie stared wonderingly at Scotland's greatest treasures. Members of the public were allowed to view them by prior arrangement, and his father had brought him on such a visit last year.

The golden crown was decorated with forty-two

gemstones and surmounted by a cross inlaid with black enamel pearls and a large amethyst. The sceptre was made of silver gilt decorated with images of the Virgin Mary. The blade of the great Sword of State was etched with images of Saints Peter and Paul, with a silver gilt handle and a cross-guard in the form of a group of dolphins. Beside it lay its long wooden sheath.

Peril adjusted her spectacles to peer closely at the Honours through the glass. "They are very impressive," she commented.

Artie noticed she was scrutinising the gems and assessing them from the mineralogical point of view.

"I've been governor of this castle for thirteen years now," said General Dundas, "and never have I experienced such effrontery. The idea that some burglar thinks he can break in here and make off with the Honours of Scotland – it is simply outrageous."

"I agree," said Inspector McCorkle, "but based on past experience, we must take this threat seriously."

"Edinburgh Castle is not some merchant's town house," said the general. "This is a military fortress with enough soldiers to see off any would-be robber."

"Any ordinary robber, I am sure," said Pendragon in his lilting Welsh accent. "But this villain possesses powers that cannot be thwarted by a bayonet or a bullet."

"Powers?" echoed the general. "Are you saying he's like

those fakirs I saw during my years in India? Those chappies were certainly capable of the most extraordinary feats."

"You have the right of it there, General," said the Welshman. "The Scarlet Phantom has learned to manipulate the very atoms of his body."

"Mr Pendragon came very close to capturing him only last night," said McCorkle.

"He certainly thwarted the villain's attempt to steal the former Lord Provost's valuables," put in Constable Pennycook.

"I am aware of your talents, Mr Pendragon," said the general admiringly. "I attended a lecture you recently gave to the Edinburgh Psychical Association and was most impressed. Are you confident that you can protect the Honours of Scotland?"

"From what I learned during our last encounter," Pendragon assured him, "I believe I can now fine-tune my equipment to trap him in an etheric net. It is simply a matter of creating the right circumstances."

Inspector McCorkle gave his moustache an agitated tug. "Circumstances?"

"Well, at the Lord Provost's house, see, the room was badly placed," Pendragon explained, "so that magnetic waves from the earth were interfering with my etheric field."

"I note that you didn't say anything at the time," Peril grumbled.

"You mind your manners, young lady," the general reprimanded sharply. "Mr Pendragon knows what he's talking about."

Artie noticed that Rose-Ivy was drifting around the room, sweeping her hands through the air as though clutching at invisible spider webs.

"This chamber is not right," she crooned. "The energies clash, the stones cry out."

"I don't hear anything," said Ham.

"Are you telling us the treasure is not safe here?" Pendragon asked his daughter.

The girl spun round, once, twice, three times, her long blonde hair fluttering about her. When she stopped, she pointed to somewhere beyond the wall of the chamber. "Safer over that way."

Pendragon squinted in the direction she indicated. "General, if we move the treasure and defeat the Phantom's expectations, we may throw him off guard. A small, secure room would be best."

"Yes, a diversion," said the general. "Sound strategy. We have just such a place down the passageway."

"I can provide a strong police presence, of course," McCorkle put in.

Dundas glowered at him. "That army are quite capable of dealing with this. We have no need of the police."

"The general is correct," said Pendragon. "The police

were of little help last time, and if that young constable had not disrupted the etheric field by rashly flinging his truncheon, I might have captured the Phantom there and then. The best chance of success is if I work alone."

General Dundas drew himself up stiffly. "Mr Pendragon, much as I respect your abilities, I cannot leave you alone with the Honours of Scotland."

"I understand, General," said the Welshman. "If you insist on accompanying me, I agree, of course, but you must appreciate the risks."

Rose-Ivy drifted over to the old soldier and passed her palms up and down in the air before him, as though sizing him up for a new suit. "This man has a very strong spirit," she breathed. "Oh yes, his aura will be of great help to you, Da. No evil can stand against him."

General Dundas was clearly flattered and his chest swelled with pride. "There then, it's settled," he declared.

"Somebody with a proper rational attitude should be there to ensure that there is no jiggery-pokery," Peril interrupted abruptly.

"Jiggery-pokery?" Pendragon echoed mockingly. "I think your imagination is running away with you, young lady. No, you and your two friends are the most disruptive presences of all."

"Oh yes," keened Rose-Ivy, passing before the three youngsters and waving her hands before them. "We must keep them away. From them wash waves of grief, pain, doubt and anger. Oh, Da, keep them away!"

"Well, I never heard the like!" Peril retorted.

Before Artie could speak up in support of his friend, another voice cut across the room. "Yes, we've had quite enough of these young scallywags treating this investigation as though it were some sort of game."

It was Lieutenant Sneddon. He had been standing in the doorway listening to the conversation, and now he strode across the room with an air of pompous self-importance.

"Scallywags!" exclaimed Ham. "You'd better not let my mother hear you call me that."

"Lieutenant, we are serious investigators," Artie protested.

Sneddon silenced him with an upraised hand. "Now that General Dundas has taken charge of the matter, I believe we can leave the security of the crown jewels in his hands. This has been a vexing business and we are well rid of it."

"Sir, we are still in the middle of our investigation," Inspector McCorkle protested.

"McCorkle, the Edinburgh Constabulary has suffered enough embarrassment in pursuit of this Phantom. You and your young friends are removed from the case. If I find them snooping around again, I shall have them arrested for obstructing the law."

18.

The Emperor's Carriage

The next day, the papers were full of the Phantom's new threat.

INVISIBLE FIEND TO ASSAULT THE CASTLE

In his latest challenge, the Scarlet Phantom threatens to strike at the very heart of our nation. He declares that he will steal the Honours of Scotland from Edinburgh Castle under the very noses of its defenders. The castle has been closed to the public and extra troops have been assigned to render the fortress impregnable. In addition, the noted psychic investigator Mr Daffyd Pendragon has offered his services to defy the fiend. Surely the unseen villain has overreached himself on this occasion. And yet Edinburgh holds its breath!

Throughout Edinburgh, gossip about the Scarlet Phantom was on everyone's lips, and the normal Saturday bustle around the city was even more energised than usual.

Artie's mood was one of boiling frustration as he strolled over the North Bridge with Ham trailing unhappily along behind.

"I can't believe Sneddon threw us off the case," Artie exclaimed, "and even threatened to have us arrested if we showed our faces around the castle."

He aimed an angry kick at a scrap of paper that blew across the pavement in front of him.

"What's done is done," Ham declared glumly over the noise of steam trains huffing and growling down in Waverley Station. "We'll just have to accept that we can't make it as detectives."

"Well, I don't like it," said Artie stubbornly, "and I know Peril doesn't either. She was fit to burst when they had us escorted out of the castle."

"She just about exploded when you told her to calm down," Ham recalled. "What was it she called us? Deserters?"

"When she stormed off she said she never wanted to see us again. I can't really blame her for being upset though."

"Well, I still don't see the use in tramping around town like this," Ham complained.

Artie clenched his fists in irritation. "I can't just sit around doing nothing when the Phantom is planning to strike tonight. I have to do something."

Ham sighed. "Artie, nobody wants or needs our help. They've got a whole regiment of soldiers up there, as well as Pendragon and his euphoric germinator or whatever he calls it."

"They think they can stop the Phantom," said Artie, "but I have a hunch they're wrong. Doesn't it strike you as odd that the Phantom threatened to rob Mr Kincaid at noon, Mr Seaton and Sir Archibald at ten o'clock, but the message he sent to the castle only said it would be tonight, with no time specified?"

"It doesn't strike me as odd at all," said Ham. "Maybe his watch broke."

"And why, after a few relatively minor thefts, is he suddenly out to steal the greatest treasures in the whole of Scotland? I tell you, Ham, there's a devious mind behind all of this and we have to find out who it is before it's too late."

There was a long pause, then Ham said, "You know what I think, Artie? I think General Dundas is the Phantom."

"What, the old governor of Edinburgh Castle?"

"Exactly. Didn't you hear him say he spent many years in India, that he saw a lot of amazing things there?"

"Yes, I remember."

"Well, isn't it possible he picked up one or two tricks himself? You know what the most famous Indian trick is, don't you? The Indian rope trick."

"I've heard of it. Isn't that when one of those Indian magicians, a fakir, hangs a rope in the air, climbs to the top of it and disappears?"

"That's it. Now suppose the old general picked up that trick. That could make him our Phantom, couldn't it?"

Artie gave a doubtful shrug. "He seems a bit too respectable and, well, a bit too old."

"You know what they say, Artie: It's never too late to teach an old dog new tricks."

"Actually, Ham, I don't think that is what they say."

Suddenly his attention was caught by a closed carriage drawn by a large piebald horse that rumbled past and stopped a short distance ahead of them. The driver leapt down onto the pavement directly in their path and Artie recognised him at once – Rajpal Singh.

The Sikh opened the carriage door and beckoned Artie inside. It was clear from his stern expression that he would not stand for an argument.

Artie froze for a moment. Surely, even if he had unknowingly fallen foul of this man's master, nothing could happen to him here in a public street with dozens of witnesses passing by. He swallowed hard and stepped inside the carriage. When Ham tried to follow, Rajpal

Singh waved him back, then closed the door and stood there on guard with his arms folded over his broad chest.

Inside, enough sunshine filtered through the lightly curtained windows to illuminate the huge, unmistakable figure of Cadwallader Figg. A selection of candied sweetmeats was laid out on a napkin in his lap and he nibbled on one of them as he signalled to Artie to be seated.

Artie pressed himself into the leather seating opposite Figg and stared at his immense bulk. He was half afraid that if the big man were to take a deep breath he might find himself crushed against the wall.

"Well, Mr... um... Sir..." Even in the privacy of the carriage, Artie hesitated to speak the criminal mastermind's name aloud. "Do you have business in this part of town?" he asked politely.

Figg folded up his treats and dabbed his thick lips with a kerchief. "Only with you, Mr Root. I felt it expedient that we should chat."

Artie tried not to betray his nervousness, but his heart was beating so hard, he was sure Figg could hear it.

"Really? But how did you know where to find me?"

"I have my methods, sir, I have my methods," Figg responded mildly. "You strike me as a sharp-witted, capable young man. While your companion – Mr Bloggs, was it? – is entertaining, he does not have your acumen." He tapped a finger against his temple.

165

"Ham – I mean Bloggs – is a good friend," Artie asserted. "I couldn't do anything without him."

"Your loyalty is commendable, Mr Root, most commendable. I see great potential in you, and I was disappointed to learn that your official involvement in this unusual case has been terminated."

Artie was taken aback that Figg was aware of this recent development. It seemed as if he had sources everywhere.

"Nobody wants us within a mile of the Phantom's new target," he confirmed glumly.

"Nevertheless, Mr Root, I urge you to continue your investigation, even without the support of the law."

This was the last thing Artie had expected to hear from the emperor of crime. "You want me to go on looking for the Phantom?"

Figg folded his hands over the front of his tightly stretched waistcoat.

"While I do not care to embroil myself directly in these matters, especially when not only the police but the military are involved, I also find it intolerable that anyone should attempt to carry out so audacious a robbery without my permission. It is an affront to my reputation and quite unacceptable. You take my point, of course?"

"I suppose you mean," Artie responded cautiously, "that your business interests, whatever they might be, would be damaged if you were to suffer any loss of respect."

"You have grasped the matter in its very essentials," Figg approved. "Therefore I would encourage you to probe deeper into this matter and to bear in mind the following points."

He leaned forward only a fraction, but it was enough to make Artie feel like he had fallen under the shadow of a mountain.

"What does one do with stolen gems, Mr Root? One cannot sell them openly, for fear that the police might trace them back to the thief." Figg paused a moment before answering his own question. "The standard practice is to sell them, at a discount, to an intermediary. That person will then sell them on at their full value to persons so far removed from the scene of the crime that no connection will be made, perhaps even to buyers in a foreign country."

"Yes, that sounds logical," Artie agreed.

Figg raised a questioning finger. "But suppose this unknown and daring bandit were to succeed in his aim of seizing the Honours of Scotland? What would he do with them? What *could* he do with them?"

Artie thought hard, realising that Figg was waiting for him to answer. "He couldn't dispose of them by the normal means you were talking about. They're too well known ever to be allowed to turn up anywhere."

"Correct, Mr Root." A small smile touched Figg's lips.

"Please continue to reason."

"Well, I have heard that sometimes great works of art go missing," said Artie, "and are never seen again."

Figg gave a satisfied grunt and Artie went on.

"It's thought that there are some immensely rich men who keep private art collections hidden away secretly, so that only they themselves can ever enjoy those treasures. I suppose someone like that might be prepared to pay the Phantom handsomely for the Scottish crown jewels."

"Precisely, Mr Root, precisely. Individuals of such fabulous wealth are not to be found locally, however. Would you agree?"

"Yes, I would," said Artie.

"Good. Then I leave the matter in your hands." Figg rapped on the door and Rajpal Singh pulled it open.

As Artie climbed out he heard Figg say, "Good day to you, Mr Doyle – and good luck."

Artie stared at the carriage as it pulled away, momentarily stunned by the realisation that the master criminal had addressed him by his real name.

"Artie, Artie, that was Figg, wasn't it?" Ham asked excitedly.

Artie nodded, still pondering the new information he had been given.

"I suppose he warned you to keep your nose out of that Phantom business," said Ham. "Good advice, I should say."

"Not at all, Ham. He actually encouraged me to carry on with my investigation."

Ham's jaw went slack. "Really? I was thinking we could go and find ourselves a nice lunch, then maybe go back to your place and play some cards: you know, normal things."

Artie began a decisive march up the street. "We're back on the case, Ham," he declared firmly. "We're going to unmask the Phantom, whatever it takes."

Ham hurried after. "Artie, if we go snooping around the castle we're likely to be tossed into a dungeon."

"We're not going to the castle, Ham," Artie responded. "We're going to the Royal Botanic Gardens."

"Gardens?" Ham suddenly perked up. "You mean we're going to have a picnic?"

"No, we're going to find Peril. I remember her mother saying they were going to spend Saturday there."

"Artie, do we have to hang around with that girl? She's so pushy."

"If we're going to crack this case," said Artie in a determined voice, "we'll need her help."

19.

The Puzzles of Peril

The Botanic Gardens were spread out adjacent to Inverleith Row, in the northern part of Edinburgh. The entrance lodge was flanked by an elm and a weeping willow which stood like sentinels over the gateway. As they followed the broad path between rows of sycamores, Artie and Ham found themselves joining a busy throng of people out to enjoy not only the lavish greenery and colourful flowers, but also the splendid views of the city from the raised terraces.

"Do you think they give out free samples," said Ham, gazing peckishly at a display of fruit trees – damson, plum and cherry.

"Never mind about picking yourself a plum," said Artie. "Keep your eyes peeled for Peril and her mother. We are here on business."

"Why are they here anyway?" Ham wondered. "I thought it was rocks they cared about."

"Apparently Mrs Abernethy has a number of fossilised ferns and she wants to compare them with samples of living plants," said Artie.

A mob of young children came running past and raced up onto the winding paths of the rock garden. In the midst of the bright Alpine flowers, they pursued each other in a noisy game of tig.

Pressing on, Artie spotted Peril and her mother strolling past the huge bull palm from the West Indies. The mighty tree was surrounded by a stone enclosure, as though it were a live beast that might try to escape into the city.

"There they are, Ham. Come on. I want you to distract Mrs Abernethy while I have a word with Peril."

"Distract her? How?" asked Ham. "With card tricks?"

"Just ask her a lot of questions about plants."

As they approached the mother and daughter, Mrs Abernethy raised the wide brim of her straw hat to peer at them.

"Ah, Mr Doyle, isn't it? And Mr Hamilton."

Ham smiled at her cheery greeting. "People usually call me Ham."

"Ham? Well, that's a fine name," Beatrice Abernethy complimented him. "There's something comfortable and trustworthy about it."

"What are you two doing here?" Peril wrinkled her nose quizzically. "I thought we'd been thrown off the case. As if those idiots at the castle have any idea what they're doing," she added sourly.

"Ham insisted we come," said Artie, addressing Peril's mother. "He's simply mad about botany and I told him you could answer all his questions."

"Well, I shall certainly try," said Mrs Abernethy pleasantly. "So you're an enthusiast for the plant kingdom, are you, Ham?"

"Oh absolutely," Ham responded with bogus zeal. "Grass, trees, shrubs, even moss – I can't get enough of them."

"I suppose you know that they have a fossil of *Pitys withamii* here," said Mrs Abernethy. "It was found in Craigleith Quarry and is the largest plant fossil in Scotland."

"Yes, of course, the piteous wigwam." Ham looked about him and pointed at a large palm topped by a mass of feathery plumes. "I would really like to know more about that wonderful specimen."

"Ah, the *Cocos plumosa*," said Mrs Abernethy. "Let's go and have a closer look."

Artie drew Peril aside and saw her sigh as she watched her mother lecture Ham. "We have a large collection of plant fossils, you know: ferns, lycopods, *sigillaria* and *asterophyllites*, but nothing that breaks new ground. We were planning to travel down to Devon next week. There are lots of fossils there and we might perhaps uncover the bones of a previously unnamed sauroid or the shell of a new species of crustacean."

"So you could name it after your father," said Artie.

The girl nodded sadly. "If he were here, he wouldn't stand for all this foolish talk about ghosts and psychic powers. He'd set everyone right."

"I'm sure you're right," said Artie, all too aware of the sense of loss echoing in her words.

Peril's head drooped and there was a catch in her voice. "It's not fair, you know."

"What isn't?"

"If your God is as loving as you and your priests say He is, why did He let my daddy die?"

Artie was taken aback by the sharpness of her pain and the glint of moisture in her eye. He was so used to Peril being determinedly rational that it was startling to see her upset.

"I suppose God has to let us take risks, no matter how dangerous," he offered. He thought about the times his father had been ill and how hard he had prayed for him to get well again. "If He kept us safe all the time, instead of letting us be free, we'd never have to be brave or clever, would we? We'd be puppets instead of people."

Peril removed her spectacles and rubbed her eyes. "What about your friend Hamilton? Isn't he angry about his father dying?"

Artie let a long, awkward silence hang in the air while Peril put her glasses back on. At last he decided to tell her the truth.

"The fact is that Ham's father isn't dead. A few years ago, Mr Hamilton ran off and abandoned his wife and son. He hasn't been heard from since."

Peril was shocked. "That's awful!"

"It hurt them both terribly," said Artie. "They find it easier to pretend he was lost at sea to keep people from gossiping."

Peril glanced over to where Ham was feigning interest in some drooping leaves. "At least I know my daddy loved me," she said in a strained voice. "That's something I can never lose."

"Peril, if we truly love somebody," said Artie, "I'm sure we'll see them again one day."

"Really?" Peril was doubtful. "Well, I suppose if you believe in miracles you can believe in anything."

"Sometimes," said Artie, "when life is hard, believing is all that keeps us going."

Peril sniffed up a deep breath and faced him squarely. "I don't suppose, by the way, that you really came here because of a sudden overriding interest in botany?"

"No, Peril," said Artie. "I wanted to tell you that I'm sorry I was ready to give up on the case and you were right to be cross with me. No matter what Sneddon or anybody else says, we've started this thing and we're going to see it through to the end. And I can't do it without your help."

Artie could see that she was pleased to be brought back into the case. "You can count on me," she said with a firm nod of her head.

Artie gave her a brief account of his conversation with Cadwallader Figg that morning.

"I think you're right," he concluded. "This is some sort of trick being played on the whole city, though for the life of me I can't see the point of it."

"I'm glad you think so," said Peril, "but I have to admit I don't grasp how it's being done. There are so many people involved."

"Let's start with the first two robberies," said Artie as they walked around the gigantic West Indian palm. "When Ham and I first spoke with Cadwallader Figg, he asked us if we thought Kincaid and Seaton were honest men. It seemed to me that he was hinting at something."

"You mean that they're crooks?"

"Well, he would know if anyone would. And he said another curious thing: he said there's no insurance against dishonesty."

"Why, that's it!" Peril exclaimed. "You know we were puzzled that anybody would choose to rob himself? Well, that's the answer – insurance. I've heard of cases where somebody with a failing business burned down his establishment to collect the insurance money."

"Yes, lots of people buy insurance for their valuables," said Artie, "so that if things are lost or stolen, the insurance company pays them money to cover the loss."

"I still don't see what they gain by it in this case," said Peril.

"Well, in the case of a robbery, the insurance company pays them whatever the jewels were worth," said Artie. In his mind he could hear Constable Pennycook's words: *If these events are impossible, we come to the conclusion that they must not have happened at all.* "But if someone only faked the robbery and still has the jewels…"

"They could sell them secretly and double their money," Peril finished for him. "But if you were going to fake a robbery, why would you come up with something as absurd as an invisible thief, with all the attention that would draw from the police and the press?"

"You're right," said Artie. "And how does a former Lord Provost fit in? Not to mention Daffyd Pendragon and his daughter."

"I believe Pendragon has a house here in Edinburgh," said Peril. "I'll bet we'd find some evidence there to shed light on this business."

"Yes, he has a place in Broughton Road," said Artie, recalling what the Ferret had told him. "But how would we get in?"

Peril produced her lock-pick and gave a mischievous grin.

"No," said Artie firmly. "The Ferret told me that Pendragon has a ferocious housekeeper, and if we got caught breaking in, we'd end up in prison. What we need to do is get ourselves a disguise."

Peril wrinkled her nose. "I don't know about that. I'm not much for dressing up."

"Oh, that's not a problem," Artie smiled. "I know somebody who's really good at it."

20.

The Phenomenon Forms a Plan

Once Peril had explained to her mother that she and the boys needed to continue their investigation ("Remember to stick to proper scientific methods," Mrs Abernethy advised), they left the Botanic Gardens and set out for Rowena McCleary's house. Artie explained that this young actress had been a great help to himself and Ham during the case of the Vanishing Dragon, and if anyone could come up with a clever disguise, she was the one.

"She usually comes back to Edinburgh for the summer and gets herself cast in some theatre production," said Artie.

"Theatre people have a reputation for being flighty," said Peril dubiously. "I hope she's not like that."

Artie chose to say nothing.

As they walked across town, Ham insisted on repeating everything Beatrice Abernethy had told him about palm trees, including all the fascinating features of the Chinese fan palm and the Australian *Seaforthia elegans*. Artie wasn't sure if he had taken a genuine interest or if this was his revenge for being used as a distraction. When they arrived outside the grand three-storey house in Moray Place, Peril was impressed.

"This girl must be very wealthy," she said.

"Her parents are rich," said Artie, "and they let her do pretty much what she pleases."

They climbed up the front steps and Artie pulled on the doorbell. After half a minute the door opened to reveal a thin, nervous woman in a lace cap.

"Oh dear, oh dear," she murmured. "We weren't expecting visitors, we weren't expecting visitors at all."

"Good day, Miss Clatter," Artie addressed her politely. "Is Rowena at home?"

"Rowena? Oh yes, my, my." The woman shook her head dolefully as she ushered them inside. "She didn't tell me there would be visitors."

"Miss Clatter is Rowena's governess," Artie explained to Peril. In a confidential tone he added, "But Rowena treats the poor creature like a servant."

"Please don't touch anything," Miss Clatter pleaded as she led them down a lavishly carpeted hallway decorated with paintings and marble statues.

"Artie, are you sure this is a good idea?" Ham grumbled.

"You know what Rowena's like."

"I know she has talents that could be a real help to us," said Artie.

From the other side of the door ahead came a terrible, ear-piercing screech.

"It's too bad music isn't one of them," said Ham.

"What on earth is that row?" wondered Peril. "Is somebody strangling a cat?"

"No," said Artie. "It's something far worse."

When they entered the room they saw a tall, red-haired girl in a green chiffon gown frowning behind a music stand. She had a violin tucked under her chin and was forcing a series of shrill, unhappy notes out of it. Artie was quite sure they were not those the composer intended.

At the sight of Artie and Ham, Rowena dropped the instrument onto a cushioned chair and rushed to meet them.

"Mr Conan Doyle, Mr Hamilton, and another person," Miss Clatter announced them belatedly.

"Arturo! Eduardo! How delightful to see you," Rowena gushed, embracing each of the boys in turn. "It's been simply ages, but then I have been ever so busy. And who is this young, er… lady?"

"Peril Abernethy," said Peril, thrusting out a hand.

Rowena stared at the hand before shaking it. "Miss Rowena McCleary, widely referred to as the Theatrical Phenomenon. You've heard of me, of course."

"I haven't actually," Peril confessed. "I don't go to the theatre."

Rowena eyed the other girl's simple tweed clothes and stout boots. "Have you just come from a rock-climbing excursion?" she inquired. "I suppose you haven't had time to change."

"No, I just prefer to dress practically," Peril informed her. "I don't care much for ribbons and lace and other such fripperies."

"You should, Perlita," Rowena advised, fingering one of the pink ribbons in her own hair. "You really should."

Peril was about to protest that her name was not Perlita, but Artie stopped her. "She likes to call people by exotic names," he confided in her ear. "She doesn't mean any harm by it. It's just her way."

"Well, Eduardo, it seems that while I've been away at the Montecelli College for Young Gentlewomen, you've been keeping company with all sorts of new people." There was a hint of reproach in Rowena's voice. She turned to her governess. "Clatter, do fetch a pot of tea and some cakes, there's a good thing."

As the anxious woman hurried away Artie glanced around the room at the porcelain figurines and works of art brought from exotic parts of the world.

"Your parents aren't about, I suppose?"

"No, no," Rowena answered airily. "I believe they are

travelling by native canoe up the Orinoco River. They are such fascinating and romantic people, I wish I could see more of them. Still, I do keep myself busy, as you can see."

She gestured towards a poster hanging on the wall, which featured a portrait of herself and an announcement in large, bold letters:

The Alhambra Theatre Presents
For One Night Only

The

Theatrical Phenomenon:

Miss Rowena McCleary

in an evening of song, dance and dramatic recitation.

Musical accompaniment by the Corstorphine Chamber Orchestra

Wednesday, August 20th, 8.00 pm

"Very impressive." Artie tried his best to sound enthusiastic.

"If you take my advice," said Ham, you'll add a comedian to the bill. And maybe some acrobats. That will draw a good crowd."

"I can draw a crowd all by myself, thank you very much," Rowena retorted huffily. "Now, why don't we all sit down and you can tell me what you've been up to, Arturo."

Once they were seated on the soft cushioned chairs, Artie explained that he and Ham had been asked by the police to investigate the mystery of the Scarlet Phantom.

"Oh, yes, I've been reading all about it in the papers," said Rowena. "I like to imagine that he's a tortured musical genius who has been rejected by a beautiful opera singer." She raised her eyes upward and waved a hand lightly in the air, as though she were painting the scene for herself. "Heartbroken, he lives in the catacombs beneath the city, emerging only to commit daring robberies by way of avenging himself on a cruel world that has brought him nothing but pain." Her head drooped, as though in sympathy with her imaginary genius.

"Actually we've been pursuing a rather different line of inquiry," said Peril, adjusting her glasses to peer at the other girl as though she were a strange species of tropical bird.

"I don't think Edinburgh has catacombs anyway," said Ham.

Giving no sign that she heard them, Rowena glanced at the door. "What on earth is keeping Clatter with the tea? Honestly, she is a trial."

As though on cue, Miss Clatter entered with a heavily laden tray. She set out the tea things and a plate filled with cakes, then departed, all the while eyeing the various ornaments in the room to assure herself that no one had touched them.

Rowena poured the tea and Ham plunged into the cakes while Artie gave an account of their interviews with the victims of the crimes and his own first-hand experience of the Phantom's activities.

"We've also had a couple of run-ins with Codswallower Fink," said Ham through a mouthful of lemon cake.

"Cadwallader Figg," Artie corrected him.

"Cadwallader Figg?" said Rowena, lowering her voice. "Yes, I have heard of him, but he's not spoken of in the best circles, if you take my meaning."

"I'll tell you what I think," said Ham, jabbing the air with a teaspoon. "I think he's behind the whole thing. It's all an elaborate plot to make himself king of Scotland. That's why he wants to get his hands on the crown jewels."

"I hardly think he's going to get the Highland clans to rise up to proclaim him king," said Artie. "You've seen him. He's not exactly Bonnie Prince Charlie."

"No, I suppose not," Ham admitted. "The throne would probably break under his weight."

"We're actually more interested in Daffyd Pendragon," said Peril.

Rowena took a sip of tea. "Oh, isn't he the chap who chases ghosts out of castles and banishes curses?"

"That's him," said Artie.

"There's definitely something fishy about him." Peril wrinkled her nose.

"And that creepy daughter of his," Ham added. "You should have heard her at the Police Office raving on about the queen of the fairies, Queen Mab, how she steals folk's dreams and stuff."

Rowena's eyes widened. "Really? There's a speech like that in a play – Shakespeare's *Romeo and Juliet.*"

"Well, she spouts all manner of nonsense," said Peril. "Frankly I think she's suffering from some sort of derangement."

"Yes, at Sir Archibald's house she was crying out for angels and ministers of grace," said Artie.

"Why that's from a play too," said Rowena. "It's the scene in *Hamlet* where the ghost appears."

"But if she's just reciting lines from plays," said Artie, "that means she's…"

"Acting!" Peril exclaimed triumphantly. "I knew it. It's all a big fake."

"We don't know that for sure," Artie cautioned.

"Which makes it all the more urgent that we get into Pendragon's house to look for clues," Peril insisted.

"Yes, that's why we're here, Rowena," said Artie. "I remembered how you got us all into Madame Sophonisba's house in disguise when we were looking for the Vanishing Dragon. I thought you might have an idea of how we could get into Daffyd Pendragon's place."

Rowena set down her cup and touched a fingertip to her chin to demonstrate how deeply she was thinking.

"I know!" she declared. "We'll disguise you as chimney sweeps. Your faces will be covered in soot so that nobody could possibly identify you."

"Yes, that's clever," said Artie. "We can claim we've come to the house to clean the chimneys."

"All we need," said Rowena, "are some shabby clothes and cloth caps. I'm sure I have those among the theatrical costumes I keep upstairs. And we can get some soot out of the chimney."

"Do we have to be covered in soot?" Peril asked unhappily.

"My dear, if you're going to be a chimney sweep, you do have to look the part. And we'll have to dress you up as a boy, of course." Rowena eyed the other girl critically. "That won't be hard actually."

"I had a chat with a chimney sweep once," said Ham.

"He told me the secret of his art was a really good brush – one flexible enough to fit up a narrow flue but firm enough to dislodge a stubborn layer of soot."

"That sort of expert knowledge will definitely help us to pull it off," Artie joked.

"We will need transport," said Rowena as Miss Clatter entered and began clearing away the tea things. "Clatter, be a dear and send for Mr Lampkin, would you?"

Artie recalled that Mr Lampkin drove a carriage for hire and always made himself available for Rowena and Miss Clatter. He was a dour, taciturn character and Artie had never heard him utter as much as a single word.

"Did you see that smile?" said Rowena as the governess left the room. "I tell you, she is besotted with the man. If he ever proposes marriage, she'll probably faint clear away from sheer ecstasy."

"Right, let's get those sweep costumes," said Artie. "We only have a few hours before the Phantom strikes again."

21.

Digging in the Right Place

Mr Lampkin, with his walrus moustache and bowler hat, was a silent as ever as he drove Artie and his friends to Broughton Road. Rowena wore an elegant fur to ward off the chill of an overcast evening, and Artie, Ham and Peril were dressed as chimney sweeps. With their coarse clothing and caps and their faces caked with soot, Artie was sure that even if they ran into Pendragon or his daughter, they would be completely unrecognisable.

"I still say there must really be a Phantom," said Ham. "We saw him on the screen of Pendragon's whatsit machine, and there was blood on the bullet you prised out of the wall, Artie, so it must have nicked him."

"Yes, that is a bit of a puzzle," Artie confessed.

"The truth of it all is out there somewhere," Peril stated.

"It's like looking for fossils – you just have to dig in the right place."

Artie recognised Pendragon's house by the gargoyle Johnny Ferryman had told him was mounted over the door. They parked the carriage round a corner out of sight, then Artie, Ham and Peril climbed down with bundles of brushes under their arms.

"Now remember," Rowena told them, "the soul of every performance lies in confidence. Believe that you are chimney sweeps and that you have a perfect right to be there."

"We'll bear that in mind," said Artie, "but be ready for a quick getaway, just in case."

As the three sweeps marched down the street, Peril glanced back at the red-haired young actress. "She's a little flamboyant, isn't she?"

"She can be a bit overpowering at times," Artie agreed, "but her heart is in the right place. And she's certainly come up with a good disguise for us."

When they reached the house, Artie rapped on the knocker. After a few moments the door was yanked open and the face of a woman, as hard and unpleasant as the gargoyle above, was thrust out at them.

"YES?"

The word burst from her lips with the force of a cannonball and Artie almost staggered backwards. Pulling himself together, he said, "Perkins, Toft and Busby, sweepers to the gentry. We're here to do the chimneys. Mr Pendragon's orders."

"Orders?" The housekeeper's voice grated like sandpaper. "He never told me about any orders."

"He's got a lot on his mind, Mrs Woman," said Ham, "what with chasing ghosts and whatnot. Probably forgot to mention it."

"The master normally leaves these arrangements to me," the woman scowled.

"This is an emergency job," Artie informed her. "Mr Pendragon and his lovely daughter, Miss Rose-Ivy, are most concerned about the state of the flue."

"He told us that back in Wales the chimneys are cleaned out twice a week," said Ham, "to keep crows from nesting in them."

"It does sound like you know him." The housekeeper wavered.

Taking advantage of the woman's hesitation, Peril breezed briskly past her. "We'll make it quick," she promised in as gruff a voice as she could manage. "You'll hardly know we're here."

Artie and Ham followed her inside swiftly. "Yes, straight in, straight out, that's our motto," said Artie.

"Very well then," the housekeeper conceded, closing the front door. "Just mind you don't leave a mess."

She directed them to a large fireplace in the front room. The three sweeps put down their brushes and began laying used newspaper around the hearth.

"You'd best just leave us to it," said Artie, willing the woman to leave them alone.

"Yes, you don't want to be inhaling any soot," Peril warned. "Very bad for the lungs." She gave a barking cough by way of illustration.

The woman backed off and headed out into the hall. "Just make sure to let me know when you're done," she ordered as she disappeared into the kitchen.

Once the housekeeper was gone, Peril's smile was visible through the soot. "It worked!" she declared happily. "You know, I wasn't really sure we could pull it off."

"Right, Ham," Artie instructed, "you act like you're cleaning the chimney while Peril and I have a poke around the house."

"Suppose she comes back and you're not here?" Ham asked.

"Tell her we've gone to fetch more brushes," said Peril.

Artie and Peril crept stealthily out into the hall. Peeling wallpaper and a threadbare carpet showed that Pendragon had not spent much money on his Edinburgh retreat.

Through a crack in the kitchen door they saw the unfriendly housekeeper hunched in a rocking chair. She was knitting a woollen shawl and taking sips from a bottle of gin. Padding the other way, they descended a gloomy stairway to a cellar and opened the door.

The room beyond was dimly illuminated by the light coming through a high window set at street level. The bookcase on the far wall was stacked with volumes on the history of Scottish castles and records of supernatural apparitions. There were also textbooks of engineering and electrical science. A variety of tools were scattered over a bare table pitted with acid burns and chemical stains. Amid the tools were a map of Edinburgh Castle and a copy of *Bradshaw's Railway Timetables*.

Peril picked up a small hammer from the table then laid it back down. "I don't see anything to help us here."

Artie was pulling books from the shelves to see if there might be a secret compartment hidden behind them when one of the volumes fell to the floor. When he bent to pick it up, he noticed some scraping marks on the floorboards. "Look at this, Peril. I'd say something has been dragged back and forth across the floor at this point."

Peril squinted through her spectacles. "I think you're right. What can that mean?"

Artie took a hold of the side of the bookcase and began to pull. "I think it means," he grunted, "that there's something behind here."

Bit by bit he hauled the end of the bookcase out to reveal the open entrance to a hidden room. Inside was a large metallic object set on wheels, which they rolled out into the dim light. It was Pendragon's mysterious machine: his 'etheric galvanator'.

Artie took an oil lantern from the table and lit it with a match, allowing Peril to closely examine the metal casing.

"I've been dying to get my hands on this contraption," she said. She fingered a series of catches that ran down one edge of the device, releasing them one by one. "I can't wait to see what's inside," she breathed as she swung the side of the box open. Artie dipped his lantern down to lend the girl light while she examined the interior.

"There's a galvanic battery here that powers a small motor," she observed. "That explains the noise it makes. And here's a self-contained gas jet to generate light."

"Anything else?" asked Artie.

"Nothing that has anything to do with ether or ghosts," said Peril, "but look at these."

She drew out a number of lantern slides on which were painted a variety of faceless human figures in different poses and of different sizes.

"The gas light shines through these," she explained, "and an arrangement of mirrors here projects the image onto the screen above."

"So the images of the Phantom were a trick!" said Artie.

Peril carefully replaced the lantern slides and closed the machine up.

"Yes," she said, rolling the metal box back into its secret hiding place. "It's been designed to create the illusion that there's a ghostly figure in the room when in fact it's just pictures projected onto the screen from inside the device. I knew it was all tomfoolery!"

"We'd better collect Ham and get out of here," said Artie, pushing the bookcase back into place, "before that nasty woman catches us out."

As he blew out the lantern there came a terrible crash from above that sent them dashing upstairs. They found Ham staggering down the hall with all the brushes cradled in his arms.

"Artie," he groaned, "I poked a brush up the chimney and an absolute ton of soot came crashing down. It made me jump back and I knocked over a cabinet full of ornaments."

At that moment they heard a dreadful shriek. "What's this mess! I'll have your hides for this!"

"Run for it!" cried Artie.

As they rushed out into the street they heard the housekeeper burst out of the front room, screeching the most blood-curdling threats. They dived into the carriage in such a desperate rush that Rowena reeled back in shock.

"What's got into the three of you? You're not being chased by evil spirits, are you?"

"We'll explain later," Artie gasped. "Just go!"

Mr Lampkin made a clucking noise and with a flick of the reins set his faithful horse off at a quick trot. On the way back to Moray Place they told Rowena what they had found.

"He may be a faker," said Rowena, "but you have to admire his cunning. He's probably made a lot of money by pretending to drive imaginary ghosts out of a lot of haunted houses."

Back at Rowena's house, the three chimney sweeps washed themselves clean of soot and changed back into their own clothes. The whole time Artie was running through the various clues in his mind, trying to make sense of the whole business.

"One thing I don't understand," said Peril, "is that if Pendragon is up at the castle now standing guard over the Honours of Scotland, why has he left his machine behind?"

"It doesn't seem likely he'd just forget it," Ham agreed, "even if his whole act is just a hollow sham."

Artie let out a gasp of delight. Suddenly he saw the whole sequence of this week's bizarre events illuminated one by one, like a series of dark rooms lighting up as bright as day.

"That's right, Ham," he said, "it *is* a hollow sham. He has a second machine that's even more fake than the one behind the bookcase."

Ham gave a puzzled grunt. "How do you mean 'even more fake'?"

"I mean it's simply hollow inside."

"Hollow?" said Peril. "What's the point of that?"

Artie waved his hands excitedly in the air. "It's where he's hidden the equipment he's going to use to steal the Honours of Scotland!"

22.

The Secret of the Phantom

"Is Mr Lampkin still here?" Artie asked urgently.

"Yes, Clatter is serving him supper down in the kitchen." Rowena gave a sly wink.

"Good," said Artie. "We need to get back in the carriage and head straight for the castle."

"Clatter will be cross that we're upsetting her romantic plans," said Rowena, heading for the door, "but I suppose you know what you're doing, Arturo."

"I don't understand," said Ham. "Are you saying Pendragon is the Scarlet Phantom?"

"What he's saying is that there never was a Scarlet Phantom," said Peril. "I'm beginning to see it now."

"Look, there's no time to waste," said Artie. "I'll explain on the way."

Soon they were in Mr Lampkin's carriage making their

way across Queen Street to Charlotte Square.

"It's lucky Mr Lampkin was still here," said Ham, realising that the alternative would have been to run all the way to Edinburgh Castle.

Rowena gave a musical laugh. "Can you believe that Clatter got so caught up in the excitement that she actually wanted to come along? I had to forbid it, of course. She's such a timid little thing, I'm sure she would die of fright if she ran into a ghost."

"There is no ghost," said Peril, "but there is a very clever mind at work."

"Yes, a mind that has been planning this for a long time," said Artie. "You were right to suspect Pendragon right from the start, Peril. Back at the Botanic Gardens we already worked out that the first two victims were probably working an insurance fraud by faking a robbery. The puzzle was: why would they come up with a ludicrous story about an invisible man?"

"Yes, Artie, why would they?" Ham wondered.

As Artie explained, everyone leaned forward to hear him clearly over the rumble of the wheels and the clopping of the horse's hooves.

"Because they were paid to do it. We know that Daffyd Pendragon has earned a lot of money from driving ghosts out of castles and haunted houses. With that cash he was able to bribe Kincaid and Seaton to claim an invisible fiend had attacked them. Presumably he had already learned that they had a streak of dishonesty."

"I can see that the jeweller could just throw himself about in the street the way some knockabout comedians do on stage," said Rowena. "That might persuade people that he was being attacked, but what about the necklace that was taken?"

"He never had it on him," said Artie. "He'd probably already passed it on to some underworld contact to be sold. Then he had the insurance money to come, plus whatever Pendragon paid him to be part of the scheme. It was the same with Seaton's rubies."

"But you said Inspector McCorkle saw him place the rubies in the safe," Peril reminded him.

"Yes, but when he was alone in the locked room, he simply opened the safe and hid the jewels, probably in a secret drawer in his desk."

"So how did he get bashed on the noggin with that bust of Wellington?" Ham inquired.

"I expect he just scratched himself on the head to draw blood," said Artie, "then smeared some of it onto the base of the bust. Then he made a lot of noise, knocking things around the room and yelling for help, making sure he was lying on the floor like he'd just been knocked down when the police broke in."

"And what about the cards with the Phantom's warning

on them?" asked Ham. "Where did they come from?"

"Pendragon provided those before he left for Aberdeen," said Artie. "Kincaid and Seaton placed the cards themselves, though Kincaid's assistant Miss Toner picked it up and put it away, so that it only turned up the next day."

"So did those two men know what Pendragon's ultimate plan was?" asked Peril.

"I'm sure they didn't," said Artie. "That would have been too much of a risk. He probably recruited them by anonymous letters or approached them in disguise. And, of course, each time the Phantom struck it made the whole thing more credible."

"But surely a distinguished person like Sir Archibald, a former Lord Provost, would not be party to such a deception," said Rowena.

"He didn't have to be," said Peril. "He was tricked just like the rest of us. That's why Pendragon was happy to have us there when he staged the Phantom's attack. The more witnesses the better."

"But the blood on the bullet?" Ham objected.

"Yes, I did puzzle over that," Artie admitted, "but the answer is simple. He just pricked his own finger and smeared some blood on the bullet before he loaded it into the gun."

"So it looked like it had nicked the invisible man

before hitting the wall," said Peril. "It seems silly now, looking back, that everybody was in such a panic when they thought the fiend was in the room."

"That was set up by Rose-Ivy," Artie explained. "It was her job to talk in that creepy voice of hers about ghosts and spirits to create an atmosphere of terror before the Phantom made his appearance."

"Just like you would do in a play," said Rowena, "if you wanted to scare the audience."

"That's probably how he convinces rich, gullible people that their houses are haunted." Peril gave a disgusted snort. "So that they will then pay him to chase the ghosts away."

By now they were travelling down Princes Street towards the Mound with what felt to Artie like painful slowness. Crammed together as they were, every bump in the road jolted them and felt like it had been deliberately placed to block their way. As the night closed in, the lamplighters were out, igniting gas lamps up and down the city streets so that they shone like glowing green beads against the darkness.

"I still don't get what the point of it all was," said Ham, rubbing his head as though his brain were hurting.

"The point of it all was to create a way for Pendragon to be alone with the Honours of Scotland," said Artie. "He probably recognised the governor of the castle at the lecture he gave to the Edinburgh Psychical Association, and I would guess that's what gave him the idea. Knowing that General Dundas was a believer in supernatural powers, he convinced everyone, including the police, that there was a thieving Phantom on the loose. More importantly, he made them all believe that only he could stop the fiend."

"So now he's up there," said Peril, craning her head up towards the castle, "with only one aged soldier between him and the crown jewels."

Rowena gave a disappointed sigh. "Yes, Arturo, what you say sounds very reasonable, but I did so hope it would be something more romantic."

"It looks like all that stuff about a tortured musician hiding out in the sewers will just have to stay a story," said Ham. "Too bad."

"Yes," said Rowena, "it is a shame."

"As I predicted," Peril sniffed, "it's proper scientific investigation that's solved the case, not a lot of wild imaginings."

Rowena rolled her eyes. "Really, Perlita, there are more important things in life than rocks and test tubes."

At the top of the Mound they turned right into the Lawnmarket and up Castle Hill. Mr Lampkin brought the carriage to a halt on the Esplanade and the four youngsters jumped down. Artie dashed straight to the gate, where two soldiers blocked his way with their rifles.

"Off you go, lad," one of them ordered. "Nobody's allowed into the castle."

"But you have to let me in," Artie pleaded. "I have important information."

"Well, come back when we're open," said the other guard, "and you can tell the tour guides all about it."

"It's not that kind of information," Peril told them as she and the others caught up.

"Now listen here," Rowena informed them grandly, "my father is a personal friend of Colonel Torrance of the Black Watch, so I think you could do us the courtesy of letting us inside."

"If you don't leave now," the first soldier growled, "I'll do you the courtesy of showing you the back of my hand. From the look of you, it's well past your bedtime."

"Oh, how dare you!" Rowena stamped her foot angrily.

"Artie, we're just making them cross," Ham advised nervously. "We'd better go before they decide to shoot us."

Suddenly Artie remembered that he still had the letter of authority Inspector McCorkle had given him earlier in the week. He took it out and waved it in front of the guards. "Look, I'm here on the authority of the police."

The soldiers peered at the paper and the first one grunted. "It's probably some sort of a joke, but we'd better fetch Captain Jameson, just in case."

The other soldier took the letter and disappeared inside. His colleague kept a stern and watchful eye on the visitors until a young officer with a thin black moustache appeared with the inspector's letter in his hand.

"Here they are, Captain Jameson," said the accompanying soldier.

"I say, what is this all about?" the captain complained. "We've got enough on our plate with all this Phantom nonsense."

"The governor doesn't think it's nonsense," said Artie. "And because of that, he is in terrible danger."

"Danger?" Captain Jameson repeated. "What on earth are you talking about?"

"He's put his trust in that fraud Pendragon," Peril burst out. "Somebody has to warn him that Pendragon *is* the Scarlet Phantom."

The captain stared at the letter, then at Artie, and drummed his foot in agitation as he tried to come to a decision.

"Please," said Artie, "there's no time to waste! The general and the Honours of Scotland are both at risk."

"Very well, young man," said Captain Jameson, "you come with me. The rest of you remain here and don't move."

With a sigh of relief Artie followed the young officer into the castle. But he had an awful sinking feeling that they might already be too late.

23.

The Game Is Afoot

"You are aware, of course, that Edinburgh Castle is a military base," Captain Jameson stated, "and the police have no jurisdiction here. I've only let you in because you sound quite sincere, no matter how misguided you may be."

"I don't care about that," said Artie as they crossed the empty courtyard. "All I care about is stopping Pendragon before he escapes."

"What? Escape from here?" the young officer scoffed, indicating the guards on watch all along the battlements and towers of the castle. "The strongest prison in the land couldn't be more secure."

"You don't understand," said Artie. "He's been plotting this for months, maybe even years. He's bound to have a plan."

"Look, I'll be honest with you," said the captain, "we military men are a hard-headed lot and we don't set much store by all this talk of ghosts and suchlike. As far as I'm concerned this is probably just a stunt to draw attention to a forthcoming show or something of that sort."

"If only that were true," said Artie, "I wouldn't be so worried for the general. I know that Pendragon already persuaded him to move the Honours."

"Only down the passage to Queen Mary's Room," said Jameson. "The room is securely locked and there are guards outside as well as a whole squad of them in the original Crown Room, just in case."

"Look, has anybody been checking what's going on in Queen Mary's Room?" asked Artie.

"No, the general gave strict orders that he and Mr Pendragon were not to be disturbed. Claimed it would upset the etheric field – or something – that's supposed to ward off this invisible robber."

Once inside the palace building, they made their way to Queen Mary's Room. The guards snapped to attention at the sight of an officer.

"Everything secure here, Corporal?" Captain Jameson inquired. "No disturbance of any sort?"

"Nothing at all, sir," came the reply. "Haven't heard a peep out of the general or that mystic character. I expect they're having a snooze."

"There, no trouble whatsoever." The captain turned to Artie. "Now why don't you go back to your friends and find some other way to amuse yourselves." He put a hand on Artie's shoulder to guide him back outside.

Artie took one step and stopped. "You should check," he said. "Isn't it suspicious that you can't even hear them? You don't know what's happened in there."

"I told you, my orders are not to make a disturbance," the captain repeated testily.

Almost without thinking, Artie made a sudden decision. Shaking off the officer's hand, he spun round and ducked past the guards. Throwing himself at the door of Queen Mary's Room, he pounded on it with his fists.

"General! General! Are you alright in there?"

Captain Jameson seized hold of Artie and yanked him back. "I warned you to behave yourself, young man!"

He was about to drag the young visitor away when one of the guards piped up, "Hang on a second, sir! Did you hear something just then?"

Everyone froze and listened intently. This time the groan from the other side of the door was clearly audible.

"That does sound fishy," Jameson conceded. He tapped on the door with a finger. "General? Is everything alright in there?"

There came another groan and a shuffling sound, then a thud against the door.

The captain tried to open it, but it was locked from the inside.

"What do you think, sir?" the corporal asked. "Should we try to break it down?"

Before the officer could make a decision, they heard the key turning in the lock from the other side. The door opened a crack and they saw the general, pale-faced and weak, sliding to the floor.

The captain pushed his way in and helped the old governor into a chair. Artie darted inside and took in the whole scene with one horrified glance. There stood the duplicate of Pendragon's etheric galvanator gaping open to expose its empty interior. The trunk in which they had transferred the Honours of Scotland to Queen Mary's Room was just as empty.

Both the latticed windows had been thrown open, and the end of a thin rope had been tied around the central stone pillar that lay between them. Artie looked out and saw the length of the rope stretching downward over the bare cliff-face to disappear into the gloom below. He realised now that he should have expected this. Pendragon had persuaded the general to move the great treasure to a room at the rear of the castle, far away from the courtyard and gateway that overlooked the city. Here, the sheer cliff was thought to need no guarding and formed a blind side where the thief could make his escape.

"Came up behind me," he heard the general moan. "Cloth over face."

Artie turned to see a wadded rag lying on the floor. He picked it up and one sniff brought the distinctive whiff of chloroform. Pendragon had smuggled the sleeping drug, the rope, and probably a sack for the treasure inside his bogus machine.

"Where on earth is that Welshman?" Captain Jameson wondered. He was still supporting the general to keep him from toppling out of his seat.

"He's long gone," said Artie, bolting out the open doorway.

He raced past the guards who were making their way into the room after their officer. He ran through the castle as fast as his legs would carry him. Some of the soldiers he passed shouted out, "Hey, where are you going?" or "What's up, lad?" but no one tried to stop him.

Back at the gate he found his friends still being watched over by the sentries. Behind him, cries of alarm were breaking out around the castle and the sound of running feet echoed like a drumbeat.

"Artie, what's happened?" asked Ham.

"Pendragon's got the crown jewels," said Artie. "He's escaped with them down the cliff-face at the back of the castle."

"I'll bet his creepy daughter was waiting down there in Johnston Terrace," said Peril, "probably with a carriage to drive off in."

"Well, this has been exciting," said Rowena, "but by now they could be anywhere."

"No, not anywhere," said Artie. "He needs to get far away from Edinburgh by the fastest possible route."

As they climbed into Mr Lampkin's carriage, Artie cast his mind back to what he'd seen in Pendragon's house. "There was a *Bradshaw* on his table – a railway timetable."

At that moment they heard a train whistle blow from the direction of Waverley Station.

"That will be the overnight London express getting ready to leave," said Peril.

"That's it!" Artie exclaimed. "He'll be on that train for sure. It's his best getaway."

"We'll never make it to Waverley before the train leaves," Ham predicted glumly.

"No, but if we hurry to the Caledonian Station on Lothian Road," said Peril, "we might just catch it there."

Artie clapped the driver on the shoulder. "Mr Lampkin, please make best speed for the station on Lothian Road."

"Yes, yes, do hurry!" Rowena urged. "The game is afoot!"

They pulled out of the Esplanade with a jerk that shook them all in their seats. As they headed down towards the Mound they passed Johnny Ferryman, who was hurrying up to the castle in search of a story.

"Hey, where are you lot off to?" he yelled. "What's going on?" He made a half-hearted effort to follow before stopping and shaking an outraged fist. "You can't keep the press out of this! The people have a right to know!"

"We'd better make it," said Peril anxiously. "The Caledonian is the last stop before the express leaves Edinburgh and we can't possibly catch up after that."

They raced downhill at high speed, the carriage swaying dizzyingly. Their stomachs clenched and they clung on tightly to the sides of the vehicle as they rounded a couple of sharp corners into Princes Street. A pair of late-strolling pedestrians leapt out of the way as the horse raced over the cobbles.

Artie could see the smoke from the engine trailing across the sky as the train slowed into the station ahead of them. As soon as they pulled up in Lothian Road, the four youngsters leapt out, with Artie and Peril in the lead.

In front of them lay the station. A temporary timber structure with a pitched, slated roof, it was disparaged by the locals as a wooden shanty. Artie charged through the entrance and saw the train ahead, wreathed in steam and smoke. He ran for it but was brought up short by the stationmaster, who was standing guard over the platform gate.

"Hold it there!" the man ordered. "I'll need to see your ticket."

"Ticket?" gasped Artie, gazing in anguish at the train as it prepared to depart. Peril arrived beside him while Ham and Rowena hurried to catch up. Thinking quickly, he said, "Our parents are already on board with the tickets. We've to meet them on the train."

"Really?" the stationmaster cast a quizzical glance back at the platform behind him.

Like a banshee howl, the train whistle echoed from the walls of the station. The engine let out a blast of steam like the hot breath of an angry dragon, then the pistons surged into life and the train lurched forward.

"Mama! Papa!" Peril cried out. "Don't leave without us!"

Together she and Artie barged past the stationmaster and raced for the train. When Ham and Rowena arrived, the man grabbed them both. "Hang on there!" he growled. "You can't all be in the same family."

Dashing at full speed past the guard's van, Artie lunged for the door of the first passenger carriage. Grabbing the handle, he yanked it open and leapt aboard as the train gathered speed. He turned and reached out a hand to Peril, who was pelting along behind him. Her face was set in a determined grimace as she stretched her arm out towards him. As soon as she took hold, Artie hauled her up beside him and they slumped against the wall, gasping for breath.

"There's only the two of us now, Peril," Artie panted, slamming the door shut. "It's up to us to find Pendragon and stop him."

24.

The Mystery Express

"First we need to make sure Pendragon's on the train," said Peril. "We don't know that for a fact."

"It makes sense, though," said Artie. "He knows that by morning the whole of Scotland will be up in arms searching for the crown jewels. He needs to go somewhere he can disappear, and a big city like London would be perfect."

"That's true," Peril agreed. "I expect he has contacts down there waiting to help him."

"In all likelihood he already has a rich buyer lined up who wants the Honours of Scotland for his own secret collection. From London they'll probably be smuggled overseas before anybody can catch up with them."

"We'll need a bit of luck if we're going to stop him," said Peril ruefully.

"It may take more than luck," said Artie. "He's very likely armed."

Peril took a deep breath. "It's now or never then."

They stepped through the inner door into the main part of the carriage and began their search.

The train was made up of a series of saloon cars with pairs of seats running on either side of a central aisle. The seats were little more than wooden benches, and many passengers in this first car had brought cushions and blankets to make themselves comfortable. They were lit by the subdued glow of oil lamps, and Artie hoped the dim light would let the two of them pass unnoticed as they searched for the Welshman. They walked slowly down the aisle, their heads turning from side to side as casually as possible to hide the fact that they were looking for someone.

Among the passengers in the first carriage were a family with two small children who were already asleep on their parents' laps. An elderly couple had brought out some sandwiches and a bottle of ginger ale for a late supper.

The next car was the baggage van with a sliding door on the side to allow for the loading and unloading of large items. Beyond this was another passenger car. Here, a bearded priest was hunched over the prayer book in his lap. Opposite him sat a woman in the black garments of a widow, twisting a damp handkerchief around her thin fingers. Two businessmen were arguing over the price of corn and a trio of students were playing cards for pennies.

All down the length of the train the passengers appeared to be quite innocent. When Artie and Peril stepped through the far door of the last carriage, they found themselves face to face with the coal tender, which lay between them and the engine.

"I didn't spot Pendragon," said Peril. "Did you?"

"No," said Artie. "He must be hidden somewhere."

"Unless he's shrunk to the size of a mouse," said Peril, "I don't see where he could have concealed himself. The only other place he could be is up front with the driver."

"There isn't any way we could get up there," said Artie. "Besides, they would never let passengers ride in the engine."

"Is it possible that you've made a wrong deduction," said Peril, "and he's escaped by some other route?"

"No, he's here on the train," Artie insisted. "I can feel it in my bones. He must be disguised."

"Well, we can't exactly stick our noses into every face on the train to check," said Peril.

"Look, let's head back," Artie suggested. "Maybe he'll give himself away."

They had retraced their steps down three cars when Artie saw through the glass in the door ahead somebody coming towards them from the other direction. It was the guard in his peaked cap, making an inspection of the train. He glanced this way and that as he walked, making sure that all was in order.

"The guard," Artie said under his breath. "We'd better not run into him in case he gets suspicious. We don't have tickets after all."

"Over here," said Peril, pulling him by the sleeve.

They planted themselves on a pair of seats facing a plump man and wife who were slouched shoulder to shoulder, snoring blissfully.

"Pretend we're sleeping," said Peril.

They pressed their shoulders together and closed their eyes. The guard's footsteps approached, then receded as he passed them on his way to the front of the train. After a short while they heard him return and head back to the guard's van at the rear.

"Do you think we should tell him what's going on?" Peril wondered as the guard disappeared.

"What, tell him we're a pair of amateur detectives?" said Artie. "That we're chasing a psychic investigator who's absconding with the Scottish crown jewels? He'd take us for lunatics."

Peril eyed the emergency cord above the window. This was a cable that ran the length of the train and, when pulled, rang a bell up ahead in the driver's cab, telling him to throw on the brakes.

"We could pull the cord, I suppose," she said, "but we've no proof that's there's any sort of emergency."

"We'd be in big trouble then," said Artie. "We'd most likely be flung off the train."

"You know, I've been thinking," said Peril. "I didn't see anyone with a bag large enough to hold the Honours."

"You're right," said Artie. "We should go and have a look in the baggage car."

Down towards the rear of the train they entered the baggage car. By the lamplight they could see bags, cases, trunks and crates stacked up on racks on all sides. There were also some bicycles, a wheelchair and a piano.

Hands on her hips, Peril assessed the situation. "Well, we can't drag all of these out. We'd probably end up buried."

"We only need to check the ones that could accommodate the length of the Sword of State," said Artie. "Read the labels: they might give us a clue."

The tags attached to the handles of the luggage displayed the name of the owner and their destination. Taking one side of the car each, they leaned close to read by the low light of the oil lamp.

One trunk brought Artie up short when he read the label:

Reverend Wilson
Atwell, St Dunstan's
Church, London

Seeing that something had caught his attention, Peril asked, "What have you found, Doyle?"

"I'm remembering that priest we passed," Artie replied.

"The one with the beard and the big hat?" said Peril.

"Yes, he was wearing the cassock, collar and hat of a Catholic priest," said Artie, "but I'm sure something wasn't quite right."

"I don't know much about priests," Peril shrugged, "but he looked quite normal to me."

Artie slapped a hand down on the trunk as realisation struck him. "I caught a glimpse of his book and it wasn't a Roman missal."

"A what?"

"A Catholic prayer book," Artie explained. "He was reading the *Book of Common Prayer*, like a vicar would have in the Church of England. He made a mistake there."

"Are you saying he's not a real priest?" Peril cast a glance back down the train, as though the man might overhear them.

"And if he's Pendragon in disguise," said Artie, "then that widow with the black veil over her face…"

"Must be Rose-Ivy!" gasped Peril.

Artie dragged the trunk out into the open and examined the lock. "We need to get this open."

"Leave that to me," said Peril, plucking the lock-picking wire from her pocket.

She inserted it into the lock and spent half a minute twisting and wiggling it. At last there came a welcome click.

"You'll have to teach me that trick some time," Artie beamed.

Peril raised the lid and they stared at the contents. All they could see were shirts, pairs of trousers and a waistcoat, all tidily folded.

Peril gave a disappointed grump. "It's just clothes."

"Remember, Peril, you have to dig in the right place," said Artie.

He pulled the clothes aside to reveal a burlap sack underneath. A set of unusual objects bulged within. Artie and Peril exchanged excited looks.

Artie untied the cord enclosing the top of the sack and pulled it open. He immediately recognised the silver hilt of the Sword of State with its decoration of oak leaves and acorns. Peril stuck her nose in and gasped in delight.

"It's all here!" When she looked up, her smile changed to a frown. "But what do we do now? It's not like we can arrest the two of them."

Artie hauled the sack out of the trunk. "We should hide it somewhere that Pendragon won't find it, then close the trunk up. Once we get to a stop, we can take the Honours off the train and send for the police."

"You won't be doing any of that," said a shrill voice behind him. "And I'll thank you to take your hands off our property."

He whirled about to see Rose-Ivy Pendragon coming through the door. She had thrown back the widow's veil from her pale, gaunt face and her eyes blazed with a manic intensity. In her hand the long, sharp blade of a wicked-looking knife glinted menacingly in the lamplight.

25.

Beyond All Hope

The yellow-haired girl looked more crazed than Artie had ever seen her before – and more dangerous. Keeping one eye on the knife, he took a cautious step forward and tried to reason with her.

"Look, Rose-Ivy, your secret's out and there's no place to run. If you return the crown jewels now, the law may be lenient with you."

"The law?" sneered the girl. "The only thing in our way is you!"

With a horrid scream she leapt forward and made a vicious slash at Artie. He lurched back as the blade sliced a rent in his sleeve, stumbled over a briefcase and fell on his back.

"I told you to leave those things alone!" Rose-Ivy howled as she saw Peril reaching into the sack.

She charged with the knife thrust out ahead of her, but Peril had grasped the Sword of State by the hilt. She yanked the sword out of the sack, sweeping it clear of its sheath, then swung it before her in a swooshing arc.

The lamplight flashed down the length of the ancient blade as she struck the knife from the other girl's hand and cut her across the thumb. With a squeal of pain, Rose-Ivy reeled back and thrust her wounded hand into her mouth.

Peril fixed her with a steely glare and gritted her teeth. "You should never bring a knife to a sword fight."

Suddenly, Artie spotted the emergency cord and made a dive for it. He caught hold and pulled. He was surprised at how loose it felt, and as the moments slipped by there was no indication that the train was slowing.

"You're wasting your time with that, my lad." Pendragon entered the carriage with a pistol in his hand – the same one he had fired in Sir Archibald's house.

Artie felt a cold chill run down his spine. The villainous Welshman seemed to be one step ahead of them at every turn, and now he was deeply afraid of what danger he might have led Peril into.

"I cut the line further up the train, so there's no way to signal the driver. When I spotted you prowling about, I guessed you'd be trouble."

Artie saw an angry gleam in Peril's eye and realised she was weighing up the odds of making a charge at the thief. He shook his head, signalling to her not to take the risk.

"I should warn you that I'm a very good shot with this,

especially when I'm not aiming at ghosts." Pendragon waved the gun at Peril. "Now, young lady, I'll thank you to put that antique weapon back where you found it."

Reluctantly Peril slid the sword back into its sheath and closed the sack.

"I knew all along that you were a common faker," she said, her voice bristling with contempt.

"Actually, I am a magnificent faker," said Pendragon. "But wheedling money out of the gullible becomes tiresome. I've had enough of their crumbling mansions and draughty castles. Now I will have enough money to retire to some warmer clime where nobody will recognise my face."

"Oh, yes, Da," said Rose-Ivy, wrapping her kerchief around her wound, "once we sell those baubles, we'll be rich as royalty."

"Stealing is a pretty shabby way to wind up a career," said Peril. "Even one as crooked as yours."

"Stealing?" said Pendragon. "You make it sound like we're taking the easy way out. It took months of ingenious scheming and meticulous planning to set this up, to find a pair of desperate dupes to fake the first robberies, to pull the wool over the eyes of the police and that old fool at the castle. It required true cunning and perfect timing to catch the old general off guard."

"That's why the Phantom's last warning didn't mention a specific time," said Artie. "You needed to be left alone for as long as possible."

"You have figured it all out, haven't you?" Pendragon appeared oddly pleased. "I'm glad there's someone in a position to appreciate the sheer artistry of my achievement. Oh, yes, I've earned my reward, and earned it well."

"Da?" Rose-Ivy's voice was as grating as a creaky door. "What are we going to do with them?"

Her father's cunning eyes shifted from side to side as though he was considering a variety of options. A satisfied smirk crossed his face as he reached out to his right and pulled back the sliding door in the side of the car to reveal the night-shrouded landscape beyond. A gust of cool air swept in, and Artie and Peril instinctively pulled away from the dark opening.

"I believe this is their stop," said Pendragon, gesturing his prisoners forward. "Come along, you're going to have a little accident."

When they refused to move, he warned, "I could just shoot you and dump your bodies out here in the middle of nowhere. By the time you are found, I will be long gone."

"It's a big step going from thief to murderer," Peril accused him.

"You brought this on yourselves," said the Welshman. "It was your own choice to pursue me, and now you've given me no option. Besides, you might survive the fall, though I doubt you'll be in any condition to continue the chase."

Reluctantly Artie moved forward step by step, with Peril close behind. The rattle of the wheels on the rails and the forceful puffing of the engine sounded dreadfully loud through the yawning gap.

Rose-Ivy picked up her knife and jabbed it vengefully in the air. "I'll give you a poke with this," she threatened, "if that will help."

With his feet only an inch from the edge, Artie stopped and placed one hand on the side of the door. Looking down, he saw they were running along a steep embankment. With the speed of the train, the drop would very likely prove fatal. He felt his stomach lurch and he struggled to remember just one of the prayers his mother had taught him.

"Go ahead," Pendragon urged. "You're beyond all hope now, so you might as well jump."

Trying to gather his courage, Artie glanced to his right to where the smoke and fire of the engine were visible against the night. Then, further up the track, he glimpsed something that made his heart leap. Up ahead, in the path of the train, someone was swinging a red warning lantern.

"No, we're not beyond all hope yet," he said under his breath. Realising what was about to happen, he cried out over the noise of the wind and the clatter of the rails, "Peril, grab hold of me – and hang on tight!"

As the girl flung her arms around his waist, he grasped the edge of the door with both hands and pressed himself hard against the side of the car.

Before Pendragon could realise what they were up to, the brakes jammed on with an ear-shredding screech and the whole train jolted as though struck with a giant hammer. Squeals sounded from all over as passengers were pitched from their seats, while in the baggage car an avalanche of chests, bags and cases came toppling down to bury Pendragon and his daughter. The pistol slipped from his grasp, skidded across the floor and out into the night, where it tumbled down the embankment.

Then all was still for a long, startled moment. From up ahead, the engine puffed like an exhausted runner at the end of a race. Artie stepped back into the carriage, and he and Peril gaped at each other in utter amazement.

"I saw somebody waving a warning light up ahead," he explained breathlessly, "so I knew the train was about to make an emergency stop."

Peril laid her hands on his shoulders and laughed. "Well, played, Doyle, well played!"

They heard the voice of the guard calling out in the passenger carriage behind them. "Stay calm, everyone! It's just a temporary stop!"

When he entered the baggage car, he tutted at the chaos and picked his way across the luggage-strewn floor.

"There's an emergency light up ahead," he informed Artie and Peril. "I expect some sheep or cattle have strayed onto the line. We'll be underway again shortly."

A groan drew his attention to Pendragon and Rose-Ivy laid out flat beneath a heap of baggage.

"Will you two please assist the reverend and his friend," the guard requested, "while I check on the other passengers?"

"Yes, you can leave it to us," said Artie, as the guard carried on up the train, offering loud reassurances.

"Fat chance of us helping them," Peril muttered bitterly. She clambered over the piles of fallen luggage and hauled out the sack containing the Honours of Scotland.

Artie took it from her and grinned. "Right, Peril, this is our chance to get out of here."

They clambered out the open side door then slid down the embankment into a hawthorn bush. A bellow of rage made them look back to see Pendragon on his feet, struggling to disengage himself from a bicycle.

"Da! Da!" they heard Rose-Ivy whine. "Help me, Da!"

As the Welshman ducked out of view, a whistle piped up from the engine. With a huff and a puff, the train began to surge forward. Pendragon stepped into the open doorway and braced himself to jump. Before he could move, however, the guard appeared behind him and seized hold of his collar.

"No, no, Reverend, you stay aboard." He yanked the

bogus cleric back into the car. "We're on our way again."

"But I must go!" Pendragon spluttered.

"You can relieve yourself at the next station if you must," said the guard, "but for now I must ask you to return to your seat."

The door slid shut with a decisive bang.

Artie let out a whoop of joy as he watched the train gather speed and thunder south towards distant London.

"I can hardly believe it!" He gave the sack containing the Honours of Scotland a triumphant shake. "We've defeated the Scarlet Phantom!"

"I think, Mr Doyle, that we make a good team," said Peril.

"We do indeed, Miss Abernethy," Artie agreed. "But now we have quite a trek ahead of us."

They found a road running north alongside the track and set off for Edinburgh. For the first mile they were buoyed by their high spirits, but eventually the fatigue of the chase and their heavy baggage began to weigh them down.

"I wish we'd brought something to eat," Artie pined.

"Next time we set off in pursuit of a villain, we must be sure to pack a picnic," Peril joked wearily.

"It's too bad Ham isn't here. He'd be bound to have some cakes on him."

Even as he spoke, they heard the sound of horse's hooves from ahead. Coming towards them up the road, illuminated by a pair of lanterns, was a horse-drawn carriage. As it drew closer, they were overjoyed to recognise Mr Lampkin in the driver's seat, with Ham and Rowena peering out from behind him.

"Hey, where did you all come from?" Artie waved a greeting.

When Mr Lampkin reined in the horse, his passengers jumped down and rushed to join their friends.

"Artie, thank heavens the two of you are alright!" Ham exclaimed, grasping Artie's hand and shaking it vigorously.

"Yes," said Artie displaying the bulging sack, "and we rescued the Honours of Scotland."

Ham and Rowena gasped in amazement as Artie opened the sack to show them the contents.

"But what are you all doing here?" Peril wondered.

"Eduardo insisted that we follow you as best we could," said Rowena. "He was afraid that if you were thrown from the train you'd be so badly injured, we'd need to rush you to a hospital."

"That was good thinking, Ham," said Artie.

"And we'd certainly appreciate a ride back to Edinburgh," said Peril.

"By the way, Ham, do you have anything to eat?" wondered Artie.

"Of course," said Ham, pulling a currant bun from his pocket. "The two of you are welcome to split it."

"You certainly deserve it," said Rowena. "I was

very impressed by your impersonation of a lost child back at the station, Perlita. You have the makings of an accomplished actress."

"Oh, I can't see me ever going on the stage," Peril responded dismissively.

But Artie was sure he saw her blushing at the compliment.

Once they were all aboard, Mr Lampkin, maintaining his usual silence, turned the carriage around and headed back to the city. On the way, Artie and Peril told the others all about their adventure on the London express.

"It was lucky for us the train halted when it did," said Peril, "otherwise we'd have been done for."

"Lucky?" said Artie. "I don't know about that, Peril. Some people would call it a miracle."

Peril popped the last crumb of currant bun into her mouth, smiled and nodded. "Yes, I suppose some people would."

26.
The Victory Banquet

THE SCARLET PHANTOM EXPOSED

◆

The apparent crime spree carried out by the so-called Scarlet Phantom has been exposed as a hoax perpetrated by Mr Daffyd Pendragon to generate publicity for himself in his role as a psychic investigator, climaxing in the attempted theft of the Honours of Scotland. His daughter Rose-Ivy was tragically implicated as an accomplice. The police suspected as much from the beginning and played along with the deception until they had sufficient evidence to expose the whole business for the fraud that it was.

With the assistance of General Henry Dundas, the governor of Edinburgh Castle, the hoaxer was finally unmasked as the so-called Phantom and forced to admit to an act of outrageous fakery. The current whereabouts of Mr Pendragon and his daughter are unknown, but two local businessmen have been arrested for abetting his scheme.

Lieutenant Sneddon of the Edinburgh Constabulary wishes to assure the citizens of the capital that neither they nor the Honours of Scotland were ever in any actual danger.

Though the official police file on the case of the Scarlet Phantom omitted any mention of the four resourceful youngsters who had actually saved the day, they and their families were invited to the castle by General Dundas to enjoy a celebratory banquet in the Governor's House. He even allowed Ham to bring Berrybus along to enjoy a selection of delicious scraps. In this way he privately acknowledged a debt of gratitude that could not be revealed publicly.

After a splendid dinner of Highland game soup, roast pheasant in plum sauce, and apricot pudding with custard, they felt that they had been pleasantly rewarded. Mr Doyle was admiring the antiquities on display and had just begun a long, boring discourse on them when he was mercifully interrupted by the arrival of port and cigars. Mrs

Abernethy revealed an unexpected talent by entertaining them all with a selection of songs by Franz Schubert while Mrs Hamilton accompanied her on the piano.

Artie, Ham, Peril and Rowena took their glasses of fruit punch outside beneath a beautiful starry sky to gaze down at the gaslit city below. Berrybus followed them out and lay at Ham's feet, gnawing on a bone.

Artie decided to entertain his friends by reading them his latest instalment of:

The Adventures of Beresford Root

Beresford Root and Odysseus Plank spurred their horses on to even greater speed. By studying the clues and examining a map of the region, Beresford had correctly deduced that the beautiful Lady Constance Trueheart was being held prisoner at Castle McDark by the evil Captain Carlton Thrash. At midnight he would take her aboard his pirate galleon and carry her off to his criminal lair on the distant island of Tortuga.

"Faster, Odysseus!" Beresford urged his friend. "We are Lady Constance's only hope of rescue, and time is short!"

"You can count on me," the portly seaman responded with a grin. "That villain will be sorry he ever crossed our path."

"I'm not sure I care for Lady Constance needing to be rescued by your two heroes," said Peril.

"Quite right," Rowena said. "She should be able to make her own escape from the villains – just like Peril and I would."

The two girls exchanged enthusiastic nods of agreement.

"Well, it is still a work in progress," Artie told them apologetically.

They were still chatting when Inspector McCorkle emerged from the banquet hall accompanied by Constable Pennycook.

"Mr Doyle," the inspector said, "I wanted to express my personal thanks to you and your friends for all that you have done to see this case to a successful conclusion." He gave his moustache a nervous tug before continuing. "While it has not been possible to pay you the public credit you deserve, I wish to assure you that if you ever require a favour of the Edinburgh Constabulary, we will be more than willing to oblige you."

"Thank you, Inspector, that's very kind of you," said Artie.

"Yes, jolly well done, Mr Doyle," said Constable Pennycook. "I'm beginning to think we may have our own C. Auguste Dupin right here in our midst."

As the policemen turned to go, the inspector suddenly paused and reached into his pocket. "Oh, I have been

234

meaning to pass this letter on to you, Mr Doyle. It was delivered to the Police Office, but it is addressed to you."

He handed over the gilt-edged envelope and headed back with Pennycook to rejoin the rest of the company. Artie opened the envelope and read the short letter contained inside.

Dear Mr Doyle,

My heartiest congratulations on the success of your investigation. I foresee a bright future lying before you. I would caution you, however, to ensure that our paths do not cross again, for the sake of your own well-being.

With sincerest good wishes,

C. Figg

Artie passed the letter around and Ham gave a grunt. "Well, at least the criminal mastermind knows that we were the heroes."

"But as far as everyone else is concerned, the truth has been covered up," said Peril, still somewhat resentful.

"Yes, because it's too embarrassing for everyone concerned to admit how they were duped," Artie explained. "Even Johnny Ferryman has been persuaded to cooperate in exchange for exclusive rights to the story."

"It just goes to show you that the truth is often stranger than the fiction you read in the newspapers," said Ham.

"I suppose you might as well turn our adventures into stories about Beresford Root, Artie," said Ham.

"Yes. I'm not quite happy with that name," said Artie, "but I expect that one day I will think of a better one."

Rowena gazed out over the lighted streets below and released a theatrical sigh. "I must confess that this past year at the Montecelli College for Young Gentlewomen has been a bit dull compared to searching for lost dragons and chasing after phantoms."

"Well, I suppose you could be part of our detective team," said Artie, "in between dramatic engagements."

"Yes, I'd like that." Rowena glowed with pleasure.

"And I could make time for a few mysteries," said Peril, "as well as pursuing my scientific studies and finding that elusive fossil."

"Well, then," said Artie, raising his glass in a toast, "here's to the next adventure!"

As they all clinked glasses, Berrybus let out an appealing whine.

"Don't you worry, old boy," said Ham, giving the dog a scratch on his enormous head. "Next time we'll be sure to bring you along too."

Berrybus gave a contented rumble, laid his muzzle down on his huge paws, and went happily to sleep.

Author's Note

Spoiler alert! Do not read this without reading the book first!

While Peril Abernethy and her mother are fictional characters, many real-life female scientists made major contributions to geology and paleontology during the nineteenth century. Among them were Mary Anning, Charlotte Murchison and Scotland's own Maria Gordon. The huge extinct beasts whose remains were discovered during this period came in time to be known as dinosaurs.

These discoveries inspired Arthur Conan Doyle to write his classic novel *The Lost World*, in which a band of adventurers find an isolated land in South America where dinosaurs have survived into the present day. Alongside his tales of Sherlock Holmes, this is his most famous and enduring work.

If you visit Edinburgh Castle you can learn the exciting real-life story of how Scotland's crown jewels were saved, lost and recovered, and you can see the Honours of Scotland for yourself.

For more about *The Artie Conan Doyle Mysteries* and my other projects, visit my website: www.harris-authors.com

Put your detective skills to the test! Are these fun facts **TRUE** or **FALSE?**